Destiny's
Labyrinth

Destiny's Labyrinth

A Novella

Dedication

To the brave men and women who are breaking generational curses and passing on generational blessings. You are the real alchemists.

Preface

In the heart of the city, a labyrinth of concrete and chaos unfolds, where life teeters on the edge of survival. This urban expanse, veined with cracked pavements and neon-lit skies, presents a dual nature: one of decay *versus* flashes of unexpected beauty. Here, graffiti-laden walls speak in vibrant hues, telling tales of dreams clutched tightly amidst the grit of reality. The skyline, a jagged silhouette against a dusk-drenched canvas, houses both hope and hardship under its expansive umbrella.

Within this landscape, the echoes of dreams intertwine with the whispers of reality, forging a delicate dance between fate and choice. Each soul navigating these streets is permanently shaped by the environment they inhabit, sculpted by the relentless challenges that define their existence. Yet, within the roar of the city's relentless pulse, a quiet revelation emerges—the profound power of free will.

Like alchemists of old, the city's residents are tasked with transforming the base elements of their existence into something divine. It is a journey fraught with challenges, where the alchemy of self-discovery becomes their greatest quest. For in these trials of life, their choices hold the potential to reshape not only their own destinies but also the legacies of generations to come.

And love—the most potent elixir of them all—casts its profound glow across the cityscape. Its presence or absence colors the very fabric of their beings. The love received in the formative years becomes the lens through which they view the world, shaping perceptions and guiding actions. It is through the lens of parental love, or its absence, that they learn to navigate the complexities of human connection, for better or for worse.

Yet, amidst the trials and tribulations of their journey, there exists a glimmer of hope—the opportunity to break the chains of generational trauma and forge a new path forward. Sometimes, they find themselves called upon to be the catalysts of change, the harbingers of a brighter tomorrow. At other times, they stand at the crossroads, bearing witness as others carry the torch of transformation.

And there, leaning against the cool metal of a bridge overlooking the churning river below, stands Ricky. His eyes, a reflection of the city lights, scan the horizon. The weight of his past choices hangs heavily upon him as the city breathes around him—a living entity echoing his inner turmoil. Tonight, he ponders the delicate balance of destiny and free will, wondering how much of his path was chosen for him and how much he carved out on his own. As the city whispers its tales of survival and transformation, Ricky stands at the precipice of his own metamorphosis, poised to dive into the unknown depths of his journey through the labyrinth of life.

As you embark upon this journey through the labyrinth of life, remember: you are both the architect and the masterpiece, the alchemist and the gold. And in your hands lies the power to shape not only your own destiny but the destiny of generations yet unborn.

1

Fresno, CA

"He's gotta show up, right?" six-year-old Ricky whispered, his voice lost beneath the hustle of their lively neighborhood. Shaun didn't answer, his gaze fixed on the street below, searching for the familiar sight of their dad's old Chevy. As the day's light waned, casting deep shadows across their cramped apartment, it became painfully clear: their father wasn't coming. Again.

The room felt smaller as dusk approached, the air tinged with the savory scents of street vendors cooking nearby—the aroma of roasted corn and fried plantains wafting through the open window. Laughter and lively music from the streets mixed with the hum of city life, weaving a vibrant yet tenuous urban fabric, rich in color but frayed in its guarantees.

Ricky, feeling the sting of another letdown, moved away from the window. He grabbed his favorite Hot Wheel—a 1968 Mercury Cougar—and traced paths along the sill, pretending each turn was a new beginning. "D'you think Dad's really gonna come this time?" he asked, his voice a mix of hope and hesitation.

Shaun, sitting on their threadbare couch, kept his eyes on the street. "He said he would," he replied softly, but his tone held little conviction. They'd been through this too many times—promises made and broken—but hope, stubborn and resilient, lingered in Ricky's heart.

The morning had started with excitement as they imagined the day ahead—playing catch, eating ice cream, laughing together like they used to. But as hours passed, each glance out the window grew more doubtful, the weight of reality pressing down harder.

Their mother, Linda, observed quietly from the kitchen, her face etched with the fatigue of repeated disappointments. Petite, with light creamy skin that still held a faint glow despite the years of struggle, she had a grace about her that belied the weight she carried. Her dark brown curly hair, always kept straight to maintain the image she worked so hard to preserve, framed her face as she watched her sons. She knew this dance all too well—hope pitted against reality. And as she watched their spirits sink with the sun, her heart broke for them. She remembered too clearly the pain of discovering her husband's betrayals, the nights of whispered lies, and the final, terrifying threat that had driven her to flee with her boys, seeking something resembling peace.

Now, standing in the dim light of their kitchen, Linda's resolve hardened. "Boys, it's time," she called, her voice steady despite the tremble she felt. "Let's get ready for bed." Ricky and Shaun moved reluctantly, their young faces shadowed by disappointment. As they brushed their teeth, the silence between them was thick, each reflecting on the empty promises that seemed to define their relationship with their father.

In their small, shared bedroom, the dim light from a single lamp cast long shadows across the walls, mirroring the boys' somber moods. Shaun, older by a couple of years and often the protector, broke the silence. "Ricky, you awake?" he whispered, his concern palpable.

"Yeah," came the soft reply, heavy with unspoken feelings.

Shaun, trying to lift the mood, suggested, "How about a bike ride tomorrow? We can head down to the pizza place, count some cool cars along the way. Maybe spot your dream ride." A faint smile flickered across Ricky's face, the first in hours. "Okay," he agreed, his voice still tinged with sadness but brighter now with the prospect of a new day with Shaun, away from the shadows of their father's choices.

Their conversation drifted into plans for the next day, slowly replacing the sting of disappointment with cautious optimism. As they talked, Ricky's eyes were drawn to an old picture of their father on the dresser. In the photo, their dad, young and smiling, looked like someone from another life. He was a handsome man—well-dressed, his clothes always pressed just right, giving off an effortless sense of style. His dark hair, wild and untamed, added to his charm, contrasting with the sharp lines of his jaw and the piercing intensity in his eyes. His face held a rugged elegance, the kind that could draw people in with ease, but behind that handsome smile, there was always something more—something distant, almost untouchable.

Shaun followed Ricky's gaze, his voice dropping to a whisper. "You know, he wasn't always like this. Things, life...

it changes people." Ricky nodded, his thoughts deepening. "Yeah, but why does it change some people so much?" He couldn't understand, not yet, how the bright-eyed man in the photo could become the source of their deepest hurts.

The brothers lay in the dim room, the city's distant sounds a backdrop to their quiet contemplation. In the simple act of planning a day just for themselves, they found a small, precious freedom—a momentary escape from the labyrinth of their father's making.

2

As the first light of Saturday washed over the neighborhood, the smell of chorizo and potatoes sizzling on the stove nudged Ricky awake. The familiar scent was a weekend herald that permeated every corner of their modest home, signaling the start of another traditional family breakfast. With a slow, reluctant stretch, Ricky left the warmth of his bed, drawn irresistibly by the aroma that promised much more than just food.

He padded softly into the kitchen, his movements languid, as if moving through a dream. His thoughts were distant, preoccupied with the burdens that had nestled deeply within him. His mother stood at the stove, lost in her own ritual, humming a melody that seemed to drift from a forgotten time, echoing a tune Ricky's abuelita used to sing. She was so engrossed in her cooking that she didn't immediately notice Ricky's pensive silence or the troubled gaze that seemed to look right through the familiar walls of their home.

"Good morning, Mijo," Linda's gentle voice eventually broke through his reverie, her words pulling him back to the present. Startled slightly, Ricky blinked and managed a faint, dutiful smile, masking the storm of thoughts behind a facade of calm. "Are you hungry?" she inquired, her eyes reflecting a mix of maternal warmth and concern.

Before Ricky could muster a reply, she placed a lovingly prepared plate in front of him, whispering, "I made it with love." That phrase, weighted with years of meaning, softened him as it always did. Memories flooded back; he was once again a little boy standing on a stool by the counter, his small hands eager to stir or taste, reminding his mom, "Don't forget to put love in it." She'd laugh and reach for a small porcelain jar amusingly labeled "LOVE," pretending to sprinkle its contents into their meal. It had seemed like magic to him then, the secret ingredient that made everything taste better. She would watch him eat, her eyes shining with unspoken pride, always repeating, "It's because I put love in it."

Their moment of reminiscence was shattered by a sharp knock at the door—unexpected and urgent. The sound resonated through the small house, slicing through the morning calm like a knife. Linda and Ricky exchanged a startled look, their peaceful morning disrupted.

Shaun, Ricky's older brother, rushed to answer it. As the door swung open, the world seemed to pause on its axis. Standing there was their father, Michael, more a ghost from the past than a presence in their lives. His sudden appearance was as shocking as it was inexplicable. "You guys ready to go?!" Michael's voice boomed with a forced cheerfulness that belied the years of absence and neglect.

Shaun's face was a canvas of emotions—shock, confusion, but beneath it all, a flicker of hope. This hope was what differentiated Shaun from Ricky; where Ricky harbored cynicism, Shaun held onto a sliver of optimism, perhaps because he had known their father before the chaos, before the promises became synonymous with disappointment.

Ricky, gripping a baseball that once belonged to his father, felt a familiar ache tighten within him. The ball—a relic from Michael's own childhood, scuffed and faded—was often Ricky's silent companion on mornings filled with doubt. It served as a tangible link to the man who had thrown it in laughter long before he had thrown away his responsibilities.

As Shaun wrestled with his mix of emotions, Ricky involuntarily stepped back, his grip tightening around the baseball. The leather felt rough and real, grounding him against the surge of conflicting feelings.

Linda, observing this tableau, took a moment before she spoke. Her face, usually an open book of kindness and fatigue, closed into a mask of cautious neutrality. When she addressed Michael, her voice was steady, but her eyes betrayed her turmoil. "Could we have a moment alone, please?" she asked, her tone polite but firm.

After a brief, awkward pause, Michael stepped aside, and Linda turned to her sons. Her gaze was warm yet filled with unspoken sadness. "Go on, boys. Spend some time with your father. He's here now, and today, he's showing up." Her words, meant to encourage, felt heavy in the air.

The brothers exchanged a glance, their mutual skepticism unspoken but palpable. They put on their shoes in silence, the routine motions unable to mask the tension that filled the room. Shaun, ever hopeful, adjusted his cap—a gift from Michael during one of his sporadic visits—perhaps as a talisman against potential heartache.

Outside, the neighborhood was slowly coming to life. The streets echoed with the sounds of morning: children's laughter, the distant bark of a dog, the rhythmic sweep of brooms on pavement. The cool breeze carried the promise of the sea, mingling with the earthy aroma of rain from the night before. It was a community on the cusp of change, each day a blend of old pains and new beginnings.

As they stepped out into the crisp morning, the boys noticed the subtle shifts around them—the new graffiti that claimed space on the aging brick walls, the old deli on the corner now under new management, its windows bright with fresh paint. The neighborhood was transforming, resisting the decay with bursts of creativity and resilience.

Michael, standing a little apart, seemed both a part of and apart from these changes. He watched his sons with a mixture of regret and hope, his demeanor an uneasy blend of assurance and uncertainty. "I know it's been a while," he started, his voice low, almost hesitant. "But I'm here now, and I want to make things right."

Ricky and Shaun listened, their responses a mix of nods and silence. Their father's choices loomed large between them, a shared history that was both a bridge and a barrier.

Today, they stood at a crossroads, not just in their relationship with their dad, but in their paths forward.

As they walked down the street, the early sun casting long shadows behind them, the brothers were silent. Each was lost in his thoughts, pondering the day ahead and the choices it would bring. The neighborhood, with its persistent vibrancy and stubborn scars, mirrored their own internal landscapes—places of beauty and struggle, each corner a story, each story a choice.

In this chapter of their lives, as in the neighborhood around them, the challenge was not just to survive but to decide what kind of legacy they wanted to create.

Michael's presence was unpredictable, like a summer storm—sudden and full of energy. He had a knack for appearing out of the blue, arms filled with extravagant gifts and tales of distant adventures. Each story he spun was vibrant and wild, filled with the exotic locales and daring escapades that seemed to define his life. Yet, for Ricky, these unexpected visits only deepened the sting of his father's frequent absences. Michael had morphed into the archetype of a man Ricky vowed never to emulate—a figure who shimmered brightly in moments of joy but vanished when needed the most.

The ache of disillusionment was a constant companion for Ricky, a relentless echo of letdown that no passing time could soothe. His father's promises, once bright beacons of hope, had turned into relentless reminders of disappointment, a series of unfulfilled commitments that lingered like a bitter aftertaste.

Michael's passion was the open road, a never-ending melody that played the soundtrack of his life. He was a wanderer at heart, his life a mosaic of brief, intense moments—from the throbbing pulse of late-night conflict to the transient highs of fleeting encounters, all sustained by the next available escape from reality. His guitar, slung carefree over his shoulder, wasn't just an instrument but a symbol of his perpetual quest for the next peak of exhilaration.

Amid the dim, smoky ambiance of roadside bars and transient clubs, Michael sought solace in his music. The chords he strummed formed temporary bonds with faces as fleeting as the notes in his songs. Yet, beneath his adventurous demeanor, there lurked a yearning for something more profound—a longing for the domestic bliss he observed in fleeting glimpses: the laughter of children, the scent of meals cooked with care, the warmth of a lingering hug. These visions of a serene life occasionally pierced his wanderlust, tempting him with the promise of stability and belonging.

However, these yearnings dissolved as swiftly as they appeared, washed away by the relentless siren call of the road. Michael recognized a painful truth within himself: he was ill-suited for the tranquility of domestic life. The thrill of the unknown, the allure of the next horizon, was too potent to resist, despite his intermittent desires for normalcy. His self-worth was tangled in this perpetual motion, leaving him feeling undeserving of the love and stability he occasionally craved. So, he continued to drift, pulled away by his restlessness, leaving behind a trail of broken promises.

As he stood at the threshold, watching Ricky and Shaun brace themselves to step into the uncertain morning, Michael's heart was heavy with the weight of his past actions. He understood the immense task ahead—to mend the fractures his absences had created. Each step forward with his sons was a tentative attempt at bridging years of distance, an effort to prove that perhaps this time, his presence could signify a new beginning.

The air around them was crisp, carrying the mixed scents of early morning dew and the distant aroma of street vendors beginning their day. The neighborhood was waking up, the sounds of life gradually drowning out the quiet of dawn. As they walked together, the gentle morning breeze brushed against their faces, a subtle reminder of the possibilities that a new day could bring.

3

Five years had flown by, dramatically reshaping the world we knew. Michael, a man who rarely graced the title of 'dad,' was mostly absent from our lives. Yet, it's undeniable he gave us something—or rather, someone—indispensable: Aunt Ginger. His little sister, Ginger, didn't just fill the gap; she redefined what it meant to be a parental figure for us. While Mom chased her own whirlwind of social engagements, Aunt Ginger's home became our refuge.

Her house was where rules relaxed and genuine warmth filled the air. Whenever we got dropped off, along with a gaggle of cousins, it was straight into Aunt Ginger's embracing arms. Her place wasn't about strict rules or harsh demands; it was about freedom and being loved unconditionally. She didn't have much materially, but she made us rich in ways that mattered—making us feel valued and loved. At her home, I could come and go as I pleased, lost in adventures with my cousins, sometimes staying out late into the night. No one fretted over our whereabouts, and honestly, there were nights we didn't bother coming home at all.

While I kept a distance from the drinking scenes, I reveled in the liberty and the camaraderie. Being surrounded by the easy laughter of my peers and the allure of the night made me crave a life unbound by societal expectations.

In stark contrast stood life at Ma's place. She had this way of handling business that made it clear—she wasn't about to let anyone, especially some dude, run her life. Everything around her was tight, like she kept her world on lockdown, making sure she never had to ask for anything. You could see it in how she moved, how she kept her place, everything just right, like she had it all under control.

I couldn't help but give her props for that. She didn't just wake up one day like this—it was in her blood. She came from a long line of women who had to obey the men in their lives, told how to act, what to think, never getting a shot to be their own person. But she wasn't about that life. She flipped the script, made her own rules, and every move she made was a statement. I had nothing but respect for that.

She was all about maintaining appearances, molding herself to fit into an idealized, polished version of an all-American life—a life that felt more like a carefully curated exhibition than reality. As much as I loved and respected her, her relentless pursuit to blend into those refined circles wasn't for me. I was committed to staying true to myself, living authentically without apology, whether that meant speaking out or standing silently strong. Deep down, I knew there had to be a way to thrive without compromising my essence or conforming to someone else's standards.

Aunt Ginger's and Tia Maria's homes were more than mere shelters for Shaun and me; they were the arenas where our characters were formed. While Aunt Ginger's domain offered us a haven of acceptance and the freedom to be, Tia Maria's environment provided a different kind of sanctuary—a place where structure and discipline shaped our daily routines.

Tia Maria, Ma's older sister, ran a tight ship, her home a bastion of discipline enveloped in unwavering love and care. The rules were straightforward and universally upheld: play vigorously until the streetlights cast their glow over the neighborhood, signaling it was time for everyone to head indoors and off to bed. But within this structured environment, Uncle Chino, Tia Maria's husband, offered a contrasting blend of raw, real-life teachings that deeply enriched our upbringing.

Despite battling his own demons and a past marred by drug addiction, Tio Chino was a pivotal figure in our lives. The area behind their house, where old railroad tracks lay like the scars of progress across the landscape, served as an unconventional classroom. It was here that Tio, with a mix of rough edges and profound insights, would impart his wisdom. As we played near those weathered iron rails, he would weave his life experiences into lessons, using the rhythmic passing of the trains as metaphors for the journeys we all must undertake.

The neighborhood itself wasn't easy—marked by challenges that went beyond simple economic hardship. It was a place where survival meant more than just making ends meet. Yet, his tales transformed our perceptions, making our playtime by the tracks not just an escape but a series of important life lessons. He taught us that every passing train was like a new chapter in life, and each one could teach us something about resilience and direction.

His stories often highlighted his struggles, yet he presented them without self-pity. Instead, he used these narratives to show us the importance of pushing forward, no matter how tough the tracks you're given. With each train that rattled by, shaking the ground beneath our feet, Tio reminded us that life, much like the tracks, is often laid out before us, but we have the power to choose how we navigate it. Tio Chino's presence was a testament to the beauty of flawed humanity. His life wasn't one of unblemished virtue, but it was real and raw, and it was filled with lessons about enduring and overcoming. Despite the neighborhood's harsh realities, our times by those tracks became some of our happiest memories, all thanks to the gritty wisdom and the unexpected tenderness we received.

"Life's like these train tracks, mijo," he'd intone, his voice as rough as the gravel under our feet. "Sometimes it's smooth, sometimes it's littered with obstacles. But remember, every challenge is a lesson. It's not about dodging the hurdles; it's about learning to navigate them."

On the other hand, Aunt Ginger, with her vivid stories and boundless spirit, painted our childhoods with strokes of wonder and intrigue. She often regaled us with tales of the eccentric old lady next door, whom she playfully claimed was a witch. The mystery surrounding this neighbor and her peculiar antics became a source of fascination for us. One Halloween, fueled by Aunt Ginger's tales, we dared to visit the 'witch's' house. To our surprise, the old woman welcomed us with warmth and kindness, offering treats and stories that turned our fear into fascination.

Our grandfather, Aunt Ginger's father, was a figure larger than life yet shadowed by his vices. He would line up chairs in their living room, performing heartfelt serenades of Mexican ballads as if to an audience of hundreds, with a bottle of tequila his constant companion. These midnight concerts, born from loneliness and drinking, were his way of clinging to a past filled with applause and adoration. His nights often ended not on the stage but wandering the town in search of forgotten dreams and fleeting connections.

These experiences, layered with the lessons learned under Tia Maria and Tio Chino's guidance, shaped Ricky and me profoundly. They taught us the value of authenticity and resilience, showing us that the true strength of a person lies not in how well they conform, but in how bravely they walk their own path—even if it's as rugged and twisted as old railroad tracks. Our childhood, woven together from tales of whimsy, songs of sorrow, and life lessons shouted over the roar of trains, instilled in us a resilience that prepared us to face the world on our own terms, embracing its vastness with open hearts and unyielded spirits.

4

In the blazing heat of '81, while Shaun was bouncing between Fresno and Sacramento, attempting to mend things with our old man, Michael, I found myself riding shotgun with Ma, shifting our lives from Fresno to Sacramento. Yet, my heart kept tugging me back to Aunt Ginger's, like a homing beacon pulling me toward the comfort of the familiar.

Ma's relentless hustle finally paid off when she landed a significant role in Sacramento, working on an innovative project designed to support struggling mothers. This breakthrough was her dream come true—a chance to really make a difference. Her enthusiasm was contagious; she dove into the project with everything she had, becoming a symbol of determination and hope not just for the community but especially for her boys.

Settling into Sacramento, especially our new neighborhood in Oak Park, took some adjusting. Lounging on our porch, soaking in the unique vibe, I couldn't help but draw parallels between here and Aunt Ginger's. "It's got character, ya know? It's real," I would tell Ma. Despite her initial reservations, Oak Park's authenticity made it feel like we could really belong.

Oak Park itself was a vibe—a playground of endless possibilities, every corner echoing a past life. The area reminded me so much of Aunt Ginger's place: a little rough around the edges but brimming with unconditional love and the freedom to just be.

Yet, as I began to meld into the fabric of our new community, Ma's concerns grew. She saw how easily I charmed my way into the neighborhood, my natural charisma a double-edged sword. Underneath her pride was a palpable fear—that the allure of the streets, so inviting and relentless, might ensnare me.

Our new garage became a mysterious cache of tires, car parts, and boxes that seemed to multiply overnight. Whenever Ma questioned us—"What is all of this stuff?"—

Shaun and I played dumb before admitting a friend had lent them to us. This only led to a new barrage of concerns from Ma about these mysterious friends and what kind of influence they were on us.

Ma often mused that I could have been an engineer or mechanic, given my knack for dismantling things and putting them back together. But my skills were less about constructive assembly and more about satiating curiosity—I had test-driven more cars than most could name, license or not.

That night, with Shaun back in town and Ma fast asleep, we slipped out to clear our heads with a smoke around the block. That's when I spotted it—a sleek, red Firebird I hadn't seen before. The urge to feel its power under my command was irresistible. Shaun, knowing that look in my eyes, chuckled, "Man, you're crazy. You always wanna push it."

"I just gotta see what it's about," I said, already moving toward the car. Realizing we'd need another round for the road, I sent Shaun back for more weed. He tiptoed inside, thinking he was silent but fumbling loudly enough to rouse Ma.

～

Shaun:

"I was creeping through the house, thinking I was slick. But Ma's got those mom instincts. 'Shaun? What are you doing?' she asked.

'Nothing, Ma,' I muttered, my voice calm but my heart racing.

'Well, you're doing something, and you're being loud. What is that smell? And where's your brother? What's wrong with your eyes?'

Just then, the roar of an engine cut through the night. Ma's eyes widened, and she darted outside."

∼

Ricky:

Seeing Ma's face—shock morphing into anger—I knew I'd crossed a line, but I couldn't stop now. I floored the Firebird, the thrill of the chase eclipsing reason.

Returning the car a few blocks away, I sneaked back, bracing for the fallout. Ma was waiting, arms crossed, fury written all over her. "Ricky, what the hell were you thinking?"

"I just wanted to take it for a spin, Ma. I wasn't gonna do anything bad."

"You could've gotten arrested, or worse! You're smarter than this, Ricky. Why do you keep doing these things?"

Shaun tried to diffuse the tension. "Ma, we're just trying to have some fun. We're careful, I swear."

But Ma was having none of it. "Fun? This isn't fun. This is reckless. I worry about you boys every day. You need to think about your future."

The weight of her words settled heavily between us. The rest of the night passed in tense silence, the air thick with unspoken regrets. Ma eventually retreated to bed, leaving Shaun and me to ponder our choices. We knew we had to be smarter, to find safer ways to satisfy our adventurous spirits. Yet, the pull of the streets was a siren song, hard to ignore. We were young, driven by the rush of the moment, always on the brink of the next thrill, the next escape. But through it all, Ma's words echoed in our minds—a reminder of the fine line we walked between youthful indiscretion and the harsh realities of the world outside.

5

It was early September in Sacramento, and my first year of high school was kicking off. The idea of actually showing up and giving it a real shot crossed my mind more than once. The thought didn't exactly get me hyped—dreaming of diplomas hanging on walls wasn't my style. But Ma? She'd be over the moon to see me graduate. She had pushed me through middle school, always on about my future, insisting I was too smart not to make something of myself. She didn't get that suits, taxes, and taking orders weren't my style. I had bigger dreams, and one day I'd show her by giving her the world. But for now, I just had to walk into that school.

Monday morning, as I walked toward the towering, slightly worn-out building with its sprawling campus buzzing with students, I heard the eager steps and the random bursts of laughter and banter of everyone gearing up for their first day. Memories of past disappointments crept in, like that time in elementary back in Fresno when Ma couldn't make it to the school's ice cream social, and Michael had promised to be there. I'd bragged to everyone about it. But as the hours ticked by, he never showed. Ma picked me up instead, her arrival stirring a whirlwind of emotions—I was grateful yet gutted. Why couldn't he just show up? It felt like he'd probably miss even my funeral.

School felt like a mix of promise and a prison, its walls echoing with the laughter and rebellious secrets of generations. The scent of fresh paint mingled with the musty aroma of old lockers, a stark reminder of both new beginnings and the monotony of school life.

Sacramento felt like a fresh start. I didn't know anyone, but that never bothered me. I managed a whole day at school, which felt like a marathon. As the final bell neared, my attention was snagged by the sickest car I'd ever seen—a powder blue '90 Suzuki Samurai with a monochrome LV hard top that gleamed under the sun. Cars were my thing since I was a kid, roaming the streets with my cousin, learning to hotwire at 11, and parting out cars by 13. There was something about the intricacies of a car that captivated me. That Samurai was a bolt of lightning, reigniting my real desires, far from textbooks and classrooms.

Curiosity piqued, and I glanced up, spotting a big dude behind the wheel of the car, rocking a long braid like mine. For a second, it felt like I was staring at my future self. Next to him sat my boy Dale. I approached, and Dale introduced me to Jason. Jason seemed cool, but I kept my guard up—you never really know someone until you've seen their hustle. I figured I'd dig up more about him later.

After school, Dale and I headed back to my place. I had just upgraded my mixing table, moving from some old equipment I'd found in the garage to my own setup. That equipment, though—it had been sitting there for years, left behind by Michael. Funny enough, that was probably the only good thing that ever came from him. I wasn't looking to be a DJ at first, but my love for music? That was always there. I started messing with those dusty turntables, making beats, and before I knew it, DJing just became my thing.

I had a gig coming up at a friend's party that weekend, and I couldn't wait to show off my new setup. The energy I felt behind the turntables was like nothing else. When I was mixing tracks, setting the mood for the night, it felt like I was in control of something bigger than myself. Dale left after a few hours, but I was still wired—my mind spinning with ideas of how I could hustle harder, push further.

Ma was in the kitchen, the smell of her cooking pulling me out of my thoughts. She was always trying to keep me grounded, make sure I didn't lose myself in the grind. Her voice carried that familiar mix of hope and worry when she asked about my day.

"It was alright," I said, doing my best to keep things light. I wasn't about to tell her how much pressure I was putting on myself to make something happen. She ruffled my hair, her touch warm, but her eyes told me she knew I was carrying more than I let on.

"You're smart, you know that?" she said, her voice gentle but steady. "You can do anything you set your mind to."

She didn't know how deep my love for music ran or how DJing had turned into something bigger than just a side hustle. But her words stuck. She was right—I could make something out of anything I was passionate about. And I was about to.

We had a gig coming up at a friend's party that weekend, and I couldn't wait to test out my new equipment. The room felt alive when I was behind the turntables, mixing tracks, setting the vibe. Dale left after a few hours, but my mind kept racing—thinking about going harder, hustling more, leveling up in every way I could.

Ma was in the kitchen, the smell of her cooking filling the air, pulling me away from my thoughts. She was trying to get me to stay home, keep me grounded. Her voice had that familiar mix of hope and worry when she asked about my day.

"It was alright," I replied, trying to mask the whirlwind in my head. She ruffled my hair, her touch warm, but her eyes held that clouded look of concern I'd seen a hundred times.

"You're smart, you know that?" she said, her voice soft but firm. "You can do anything you set your mind to." She didn't know how hard I was pushing myself, juggling so much just to keep things moving. But in that moment, her words stuck with me. She was right. I could make something out of anything—and I was going to.

"I know, Ma," I forced a smile, but inside, I was restless. Today's glimpse of that powder blue ride had shown me a life far from school hallways.

That night, as I lay in bed, my mind raced with dreams of making it big, of cruising in a ride like Jason's, living on my terms, giving Ma the life she deserved. Her words echoed in my head, a mantra of hope and expectation.

The next day, my focus wasn't on school. I watched the clock, counting down to freedom. When the bell rang, I was the first out the door, rushing to meet Dale. "So, what's the deal with Jason?" I asked, trying to sound casual. Dale grinned, leaned in, and said, "He's been in the game a while. Runs things smooth, knows how to keep money flowing."

That was it. That was the life I wanted. School was just a stepping stone, or maybe a stumbling block.

The weekend arrived, and setting up my mixing table for the party, I felt a buzz of excitement. Music was my escape, my way to express, to be seen. The party was a hit, and for those hours, I was in my element, away from the doubts and the drudgery of school life.

Lying in bed later that night, I made up my mind. I'd stick with school, if only to keep Ma off my back, but my real focus would be on the hustle—learning from cats like Jason, making connections, and building the life I envisioned. I had dreams, and no classroom was going to hold me back.

Days turned into weeks, and I found myself straddling two worlds. By day, a student doing just enough to stay under the radar; by night, a hustler on the streets, spinning tracks and picking up tips from the vets. It wasn't easy, balancing the dual lives, but it felt right. I was crafting my future, my way. School was just a backdrop, another part of the city's scenery. My real education was out there, in the hustle, in the grind. As long as I stayed sharp, stayed hungry, I knew I'd make it—for me, for my future, for Ma.

6

"Ring, ring, ring!" The phone echoed through the living room, cutting through the hazy quiet that had settled over the room. Shaun was sprawled out on the couch, teetering on the edge of sleep, but the sharp sound yanked him back. His body felt heavy, sinking deeper into the cushions, and he wasn't ready to let go of the numbness that had been his companion. Whatever Ricky had been involved in lately, it was potent—enough to make him scarce, though that was nothing new. Both brothers were caught up in their own lives, running with different crowds, trying to get by. Yet, despite Ricky's absence, Shaun couldn't shake a sense of pride in how his brother always handled things with a quiet determination.

The phone kept ringing, cutting through the quiet of the living room. Shaun lay sprawled on the couch, teetering on the edge of sleep, when Ma's voice suddenly filled the room, sharp and panicked. "WHAT?! WHAT'S GOING ON?!" Her voice cracked, the fear unmistakable. It wasn't one of her usual freakouts over neighborhood drama or gossip from the old ladies down the block. This was different—there was real fear in her tone, and it clutched Shaun's chest like a vice.

He sat up, shaking off the last remnants of his daze, trying to focus. Ma was pacing the living room, her footsteps heavy on the worn-out carpet. The room, dimly lit by the flickering TV playing some late-night rerun, seemed to close in on itself, suffocating. The drawn curtains did little to muffle the distant hum of the city, a reminder that life outside kept moving, even while it felt like their world had come to a halt.

Ma's voice rose again, cutting through the tense air. She was hollering now about the kids Ricky had been hanging with, swearing they were no good, but there was no way that sweet boy Andrew was mixed up in it. Shaun felt his stomach twist—anger and dread bubbling up inside him. He should have seen this coming, should've known something was off when Ricky started hanging with those new faces. But Ricky was smart—smarter than most gave him credit for. He was careful, always had been. That's why none of this made sense.

Now, here's the thing about Ma. She had a habit of making snap judgments. She'd see a kid in baggy jeans, hoodie up, and she'd already have them figured out in her mind, like their whole life story was written in the way they dressed. Sometimes, she was spot on, but more often than not, she missed the mark. Tonight, though, Shaun couldn't shake the feeling that maybe—just maybe—she was right.

Then it hit him. Ricky was in some serious trouble. The cops had him in holding, claiming he'd been ordering things off QVC with stolen credit cards and shipping the goods to Andrew's house. That didn't sound like Ricky. His little brother wasn't sloppy like that, and he sure as hell wouldn't be dumb enough to send stolen goods to a place where he was known. That was just asking to get caught. But if the cops were involved, it was bigger than some neighborhood beef or a schoolyard prank. This was real, and it had teeth.

The phone rang again, insistent and shrill. Ma, still worked up, snatched it up, snapping, "WHAT?!" This time, it was Andrew's old man on the line. His voice was low and steady, clearly trying to smooth things over with a few calm words. He was explaining how the cops had come knocking at their door that afternoon, questioning the boys about packages stacked up in the house. And Andrew, scared out of his mind, admitted they were his. Next thing, he's in cuffs. But when the cops pressed him, asking if anyone helped, Andrew threw Ricky's name into the mix.

Andrew had it easy. He had a lawyer for a dad, so he thought he could wiggle out of anything. It's how it worked—kids like Andrew, white with connections, could pull stunts like this and walk away clean. But for kids like Ricky and Shaun, they were screwed before they even had a chance to explain. Now, Andrew's old man was on the phone, kissing up to Ma, insisting it was all a misunderstanding and that Ricky was free to go. He promised it wouldn't happen again, acting all shocked that his perfect son could be involved in something shady.

Ma was in shock. She couldn't believe that this clean-cut, well-off white kid would drag Ricky into something like this. But that was the thing—people like Andrew knew how to play the game, and Ricky, well, he was always too loyal for his own good. He couldn't turn his back on a friend, even when they didn't deserve it.

When Ma headed to the station to pick Ricky up, Shaun was left alone in the living room, the silence pressing down on him like a weight. His mind raced—how had things gotten this twisted? Ricky was always the solid one, keeping his head down and doing what he needed to do. But now, he was caught up in something that could stick with him forever. The streets didn't care how smart you were. They'd chew you up and spit you out without a second thought.

Shaun got up, pacing the small space. The walls seemed to close in on him, the faded family photos staring down like ghosts of simpler times. Times when it was just him and Ricky, two brothers against the world. But those days were long gone, buried under the weight of everything they'd been through.

When Ma finally returned, Ricky was with her, wearing that cocky grin like he'd just pulled off the greatest trick of all time. He threw out a half-hearted apology, "Sorry, Ma. Didn't mean to worry you, but Andrew was scared. You know he can't handle something like that on his own. He didn't mean any harm."

Shaun could see through the act, though. Ricky was playing it cool, but there was a tension in his eyes, a tightness in his jaw that told Shaun he was shaken, even if he wouldn't admit it. And that scared him more than anything.

That was the thing about Ricky—he was ride or die. If you needed someone to watch your back, Ricky was your guy. He'd been that for Shaun since day one, probably the only person Shaun could ever trust like that. And yeah, Shaun was the older brother, supposed to be the one looking out for Ricky, but half the time, it felt like Ricky was the one protecting him—willing to take risks for the people he cared about, no matter what.

To Ma, Ricky was still the baby of the family, and in her eyes, he could do no wrong. Maybe that was part of the problem. She couldn't see the side of Ricky that was out there taking the heat for people who wouldn't do the same for him. That was Ricky—he had a good heart, even when it led him into trouble. And that good heart? It was going to get him hurt one day if he wasn't careful.

Shaun watched as Ma fussed over Ricky, her hands fluttering around him like she was trying to make sure he was still all in one piece. Ricky kept smirking, playing it off like it was no big deal, but Shaun knew better. He knew Ricky better. And as Shaun stood there, leaning against the doorframe, he couldn't shake the weight in his chest, that gnawing fear that just wouldn't go away.

As he lay back down on the couch, trying to get comfortable again, Shaun couldn't help but think about how things had gotten so twisted. Ricky had always been solid, but the world they were in? It was built to mess with kids like them. One wrong move, and you were stuck in something that stayed with you forever. And Ricky—he was too smart for this mess, but the streets didn't care how smart you were. They'd take you down regardless.

Shaun just hoped Ricky would see it before it was too late, before the streets took more than they already had from them. He wasn't ready to lose his little brother to something that wasn't even his fault. But that was the world they were living in, and Ricky? He was right in the middle of it, right where he wanted to be.

But deep down, Shaun knew he couldn't protect Ricky from everything. And that scared him more than anything else.

7

Two years ago, I made a decision—a decision to give school a shot. But after trying to juggle two worlds for a year, I realized I had to make a choice, and school wasn't it. It's kinda funny when you think about it, leaving for school every day when my mom heads to work, only to sneak back home once she's gone. It takes me back to when Shaun and I were kids, maybe 8 or 10 years old. We'd stroll real slow to the bus stop, making sure to miss the bus on purpose, then just casually head back home to chill all day. We thought we were slick, like we had it all figured out.

Shaun's been MIA lately, staying in Fresno with our pops. Now he's back, hanging with his own crew. I've been rolling tough with Jason and my homie. Jason's like the older brother I never had—tough, smart, and always ten steps ahead. He grew up bouncing from home to home in the foster system and was eventually adopted, but some things just stick with you. You spend your life trying to prove to yourself that you're worthy of sticking around. Now Shaun, he's blood, and sometimes I wonder if he's better off in Fresno, away from all this. Meanwhile, I got my first bit of work, stacking small moves until I can make bigger ones. I'm in deep now, but it feels right, like this is what I'm meant to be doing.

My pager starts to beep, and the only time it beeps, it's for money. The sound is like a pulse, steady and demanding. I look at the number and feel that familiar rush. "Let's roll," I say to my homie, who's been eyeing me, waiting for the next move. We head to the Wienerschnitzel down the street to serve someone—figuring it's the perfect time to grab a chili dog. But as we pull up, the sun's setting, casting long shadows across the lot. The place looks different in this light, eerie almost. I get this feeling, a tightening in my gut, like the air's too thick to breathe. My homie's cracking jokes, trying to ease the tension, but it's not working. Something's off, but I brush it off, telling myself it's just hunger or nerves.

As soon as I open my car door, everything seems to slow down. I spot them—the boys—rolling up in their unmarked car, lights flashing in the distance, cutting through the twilight like a warning. My homie's face goes pale, his eyes wide with fear. I can see it written all over him—he's not built for this. I should've known better than to bring him along, but it's too late now. No turning back.

They roll up on us fast, search me rough and hard, like they're just waiting for me to make a wrong move. It doesn't take them long to find the little bag of coke in my pocket—not a lot, but enough to cause a problem. Before I know it, I'm in the back of their car, the cold leather pressing against my back, the weight of the situation settling in. My homie's sitting next to me, cuffed up, shaking like a leaf. I told him a hundred times he ain't cut out for this life, that he should stick to cracking jokes and hitting the books. But he didn't listen.

Now here we are, caught up in something I should've seen coming.

In holding, the room is sterile, cold, with the smell of bleach and sweat hanging in the air. The fluorescent lights buzz overhead, casting a harsh glare on everything.

The cops start grilling me about where I got the stuff, saying they'll let me out if I snitch. The walls feel like they're closing in, but I keep my cool. I've seen this play before, and I know how it ends. I'm no rat; this comes with the territory. They keep pushing, trying to break me, but I'm not budging. When I get my phone call, I hit up my ma. I can hear the collect call tone, and then the automated voice, "You've got a collect call from RICKY." The second she picks up, I can hear it in her voice—she's about to lose it.

"Ricky, what the hell happened?" she snaps, her voice shaky but strong. My ma's tiny, but she's got more fight in her than most people I know.

"Don't worry, Ma. I'm good," I say, trying to keep my voice steady. "I just need you to come get me."

There's a pause, and I can hear her trying to keep it together. "I'm on my way," she says finally, and I can picture her grabbing her purse, already halfway out the door.

When she gets there, her face is tight with worry, the lines around her eyes deeper than I remember. She hands over the bail money without a word, her hands trembling just a little. I can tell she wants to yell at me, ask me what I'm thinking, but she doesn't. Not here, not now. Instead, she just looks at me, her eyes full of that fierce love that only a mother can have, and all I'm thinking about is how I'm about to hustle harder than ever to get her back right.

After we get home, I head straight to my room and flop down on the bed, staring up at the ceiling. The weight of the day presses down on me, but so does something else—a realization, a clarity that I didn't have before. School was never my thing. I didn't fit the mold they tried to force me into. But out there, in the streets, making moves, earning respect, and stacking cash—that felt right. That felt like me. Still, there's a voice in my head that sounds like Shaun's, telling me to think twice, to look at where this road is leading. But I shove it down, bury it deep. I've made my choice.

The next morning, I go through the motions, pretending to head to school. I wait until Ma's car pulls out of the driveway before doubling back, making my way to Jason's spot. He's already there, leaning against his car, a cigarette dangling from his lips.

"You good?" he asks, flicking the ash onto the pavement.

"Always," I reply, because that's what he needs to hear.

He nods, satisfied. "We got work to do. Let's get to it."

We had plans to expand, take our hustle to the next level. The streets were ours for the taking, and I was ready to seize every opportunity. Days turned into weeks, and my double life got more demanding. But instead of feeling trapped, I felt free—like I was finally living the life I wanted. By night, I was deep in the hustle, learning from Jason, making connections, and building my rep. It wasn't easy, but it was exhilarating. There were close calls, like the time the boys almost caught us again. We had to be smart, always one step ahead. It was a constant game of cat and mouse, but I thrived on the adrenaline, the challenge.

As I lay in bed, staring at the ceiling, I felt a strange mix of excitement and dread. The streets had a way of pulling you in, making you feel invincible. But deep down, I knew it was a dangerous game—a game that could cost me everything. Still, the rush was addictive, and I wasn't ready to give it up. Not yet.

8

"Brmm!" The engine growled as I pulled up to the usual spot, the rumble echoing off the walls like a familiar tune. It was early, barely light out, but everyone knew it was me from the roar of the Camaro. Eric's Donuts, where the owner, Eric, and I were on a first-name basis. His wife? She made the meanest ice-white mocha you'd ever taste, a smooth blend that hit just right every morning.

With my mocha in one hand, a freshly lit blunt in the other, and a pack of Newports stashed in the glove box, the day was officially started. This was the setup, the prelude to getting the money right. As the sun climbed higher, the block started to wake up. The D-boys rolled in one by one, staking out their corners, setting up shop. This was the grind, the hustle.

My pager buzzed—Jason. Didn't even need to call him back; he already knew where I'd be. Not long after, he pulled up, just like clockwork.

In the streets, Jason and I were known as brothers. We never corrected anybody because, in our world, blood didn't matter as much as loyalty. We had each other's backs, no questions asked. When things went sideways— and they always did—we knew what it meant when one of us hit the other with, "get the mask." That was the signal, the code. It wasn't just a phrase; it was a line you didn't want to cross with us unless you were looking to end up on the wrong side of the night.

Jason was a few years older, had already seen some things, lived a life that most couldn't handle. He wasn't just street-smart; he had this sixth sense about people. He could size up a man in seconds, know if they were solid or if they'd fold under pressure. But his eyes were always on the prize—the money. That's what made us click so well. We were both chasing that paper, though in different ways. By that time, I didn't really have a place to call home. Home was wherever the money took me. I was always on the move, chasing paper, or with some girl who was just as hungry as me. That was the life we chose, the life we built. For me, it wasn't about roots or settling down—it was about the hustle, about stacking bills and staying ahead of the game.

The streets respected us, not just for what we did but for how we carried ourselves. We weren't loud or flashy, at least not in a way that would draw the wrong kind of attention. We moved in silence, handled our business, and kept our circle tight. That's why, when Jason pulled up at my mom's that day to kick it with me and Jimmy, I could tell something was off. He wasn't his usual self. My ma never really liked Jason. She thought he was the reason my life had taken a different path, but what she didn't get was that I always had my own plans. Jason just happened to be the right connection at the right time. He was more than just a partner in crime; he was the brother I never had. His baby moms, though, she was always on his case, always trippin' about him not spending enough time with his kid. Like she didn't see how hard he was grinding to put food on their table, clothes on their backs. But to us, that's what mattered—providing. We didn't have fathers to teach us the game, but we knew how to hustle. I reminded Jason of that when he started talking about stepping back. I told him, "You gotta get this money first. Once the money's straight, then you can take care of everything else."

But deep down, I knew it wasn't just about the money for Jason. There was something weighing on him, something more than just the pressure from his baby moms. I could see it in his eyes, the way he avoided looking at me straight on, the way he hesitated before speaking. Jason wasn't the type to hesitate. I could tell he was questioning the life we were living, wondering if all the grinding, all the nights spent on the streets, were really worth it. And that was dangerous. Doubt could get you killed out here.

I was always in that "get money by any means necessary" mode. Connections were everything, and I had them everywhere—in every hood. Jason was more cautious, more selective with who he kept close. But me? I made it my business to know what was happening in every corner of the city. The more connections I had, the longer my paper stretched. But don't get it twisted—just because I knew people didn't mean I trusted them. I'd show up, play the fly on the wall, listen, observe. The streets were full of snakes, and you'd be surprised how many of them were hiding in plain sight, pretending to be your friend while plotting your downfall. The last thing I was gonna do was let one of them come close enough to bite me and mess up my money.

We had our crew, though—me, Jason, Jimmy, and Keith. We were tight, but Jason and I, we were different. We weren't just about the money; we were about survival. And when it came to the ladies, we were the ones they flocked to. Jason used to call me Casanova, said I had that smooth talk that could make any girl drop her guard. But it wasn't just about getting the girls; it was about making sure they were assets, not liabilities. We played our roles well, knew how to work the streets and the women in them. But at the end of the day, it was always about the same thing: the money, the loyalty, and the survival of the fittest.

I remember one night in particular, after a long day of hustling, we were posted up in Jason's car. It was his pride and joy, the only thing he seemed to care about as much as his kid. We were just sitting there, engine idling, the city lights reflecting off the polished chrome. Jason lit the blunt, took a long drag, and then, out of nowhere, he says, "Ever wonder what it would be like to just... disappear? Leave all this behind, start fresh somewhere else?"

I didn't answer right away. I just watched the smoke curl up into the night, disappearing into the darkness. "Nah," I finally said.

Jason didn't say anything, just nodded like he understood. But I knew he didn't. Not really. Because if he did, he wouldn't be asking questions like that. Questions that could get us both killed.

We stayed there in silence for a while, the sound of the engine and the distant hum of the hood the only things keeping us grounded. And in that moment, I realized that things were changing. The game was changing. And if we weren't careful, it was gonna swallow us whole.

9

The '68 Camaro purring beneath me. Just as I'm about to really let loose, my pager starts buzzing like it's got a grudge. I glance down and see the numbers flashing—"911"—from my brother. "FUCK." This can't be good.

I slam my foot on the gas, and the Camaro roars to life, tearing down the road like it's got something to prove. Anyone watching would think I was racing, but nah, I'm just soaking in the power of this beauty. She's finally ready for summer, all custom everything, from the rims to the paint job. Got her looking like a dream on wheels. Ever since I got my money right, I've been on a whole new level. Anything I want, I can have, and the same goes for anyone.

But when I'm not out there hustling, I'm in the garage, building something fresh, something that turns heads. I spend my time finding the rarest parts, the stuff no one else has, then take it to my homie's shop where we get down to business.

As I pull up to my brother's spot in Oak Park, I can see the worry etched on his face. He doesn't even have to say much. Just a look, and I know it's serious. He starts telling me how some fool came through trying to pick up some stuff, but when it came time to pay, the dude tried to play slick, acting like he could just walk off with it. Now, that's the kind of shit that doesn't fly with me. We've always been about respect, and when someone tries to get funny, it's a straight-up violation.

I ask him what this guy looked like, and as soon as he starts describing him, I know exactly who it is. Dude's been a problem before, rolling around in that old school but can't pay up. Nah, not today. I tell my brother to hop in, and we're out, heading straight for the guy's place. No hesitation.

When we get there, we don't even have to speak. My brother knows the drill. I crouch down by the driver's side door of the car, eyes scanning the street for any sign of life. It's dead quiet, just the way I like it. I reach under the dash, fingers finding that familiar bundle of wires. A quick twist, and I've got it hot-wired in seconds. The engine sputters, then catches, and we're rolling. But we ain't taking it far—just down the block to my boy's shop.

We pull in, and within an hour, the car's stripped down to its bones. Hood, seats, rims—all parted out like a Thanksgiving turkey. This ain't our first rodeo, and it sure as hell won't be our last. Most times, we'd go straight for the guy—handle it face-to-face, you know? But tonight, it's different. Sometimes the best way to teach a lesson is in silence. An eye for an eye, as they say. Next time this fool decides to play games, he'll think twice—except there won't be a next time.

By the time we're done, it's pushing midnight, and my stomach's growling louder than the Camaro's engine. I head over to Suzie's, this greasy spoon that's open all night. Their deluxe cheeseburger is calling my name, and I ain't about to ignore it. I pull up, order my usual, and as I'm waiting, something—or rather, someone—catches my eye.

"Damn," I mutter under my breath. She's sitting in the corner, minding her own business, but it's impossible not to notice her. She's not the type that's out here begging for attention. Nah, she's too cool for that, too smooth. Her hair's short, a little messy, but it suits her. And that skin—

caramel, glowing like she just stepped out of a dream. I can tell she's got an athletic build, her muscles subtly flexing under her jeans. There's something about the way she carries herself, like she doesn't give a damn if anyone's looking—but here I am, and I can't stop.

I look her way, and the moment our eyes meet, she looks away, quick. There's something in that, too—like she's playing a game she knows she'll win. I'm just about to walk over when I hear, "Order number 22!" The sound snaps me back to reality. That's my cue.

As I grab my food and head out, I glance back at her one last time, thinking maybe this isn't the last time I'll see her. There's something about her that sticks with me, like a melody you can't shake. But right now, there's other business on my mind. I slide back into the Camaro, cheeseburger in hand, and head back into the night.

As I drive, I can't help but feel that pull, that hunger—not just for the food, but for more. More of the cars, the rush, the life I'm carving out for myself. And maybe, just maybe, for a girl who doesn't need anyone but just might want someone like me. The engine hums beneath me, the city lights blurring past, and I feel like I'm on the edge of something big. Summer's just getting started, and so am I.

10

T*hump, thump, thump.* The bassline from a passing car's stereo vibrated through the thin walls of my apartment, a low hum that seemed to resonate with the thudding of my heart. It was barely morning, and already the world was alive with its own rhythm. My phone buzzed on the nightstand, shattering the last remnants of sleep. I glanced at the screen and saw "Ma" flashing in bold letters.

"Hey, Ma," I mumbled, still groggy.

"Mijo, I need you to come over for dinner tonight," her voice was warm, yet carried that tone that said it wasn't really a request. When my ma called me over, it wasn't something you debated. It was a summons, wrapped in love and homemade tortillas.

"Yeah, sure thing," I replied, already smelling the food in my mind. My ma had this way of luring me to her house with the promise of a meal, and I could never resist. It was like she always had something simmering on the stove, just waiting for someone to knock on her door.

Hours later, I found myself standing on her doorstep, the sun dipping low behind me. I knocked, and almost instantly, the door swung open. There she was, my ma, her smile as bright as the kitchen light behind her.

"Mijo, you look so handsome," she beamed, her eyes crinkling at the corners as she pulled me into a tight hug. "Look at my handsome baby boy."

As soon as I stepped inside, the familiar aroma of chicken bouillon, Spanish rice with the perfect amount of tomato, and something else—something magical—wrapped around me. My stomach growled in response. My ma had set the table for three: me, Jason, and herself. Even though she wasn't Jason's biggest fan, she never turned anyone away from her table, especially if it meant I'd be there too.

She walked over to the table, carefully placing a steaming plate in front of me. "Here you go, honey. I made your favorite." I didn't need to look to know what it was—green enchiladas, Spanish rice, and beans. My mouth watered as I took the first bite, the flavors instantly transporting me back to simpler times. There was something about my ma's cooking that filled me with a love I sometimes forgot I'd ever known.

"Mmm," I muttered, too busy devouring the food to even say thank you.

As we ate, we started talking, the conversation flowing easily between bites. My ma wanted to know what we were up to tonight, so I told her about the gig Jason and I were DJing downtown. She listened, nodding, but I could see the concern etched on her face. Her thoughts were racing, but all she said was, "Okay, just be careful, honey. And don't stay out too late—the only thing out late is trouble."

Later that night, we pulled up to the spot. It was a small house, tucked away in a rundown part of town. The place looked abandoned, but the crowd outside said otherwise. We hauled our equipment inside, the dim lights casting long shadows on the cracked walls. As we set up, the room started to fill, the air buzzing with anticipation.

Once the music started, the energy in the room shifted. Bodies moved to the beat, and the sound system pulsed with every drop. The ladies were up front, eyes locked on us, trying to catch our attention. Jason and I exchanged a glance, knowing we were in our element. But then, slowly, almost imperceptibly, the vibe in the room began to change. The crowd split, tension rising like steam from a kettle. We'd seen it happen before, and we knew what came next if we didn't pack it up fast.

"We out," I nodded to Jason, and we started breaking down our gear. The last thing we needed was for things to get heated and for someone to pull a piece. We slipped out before the situation could boil over, leaving the drama behind us.

On the way out, my mind drifted. I should've been heading to my brother's place, but instead, a craving hit me hard. Denny's. Specifically, a BLT. It was like a siren's call, and no matter how full the parking lot looked, I wasn't about to be denied. We pulled in, found a spot, and walked in like we owned the place.

Inside, the spot was packed. A couple of my boys were already there, so we slid into a booth with them. I ordered my sandwich, but my attention wasn't on the menu. It was on her. There she was again, the same girl I'd seen around, always just out of reach. Tonight, though, I caught her looking. I would like to say she liked what she saw, but my eyes were redder than ever. Not trying to be noticed, but there it was—just a quick glance, and I knew.

I called her over with a crook of my finger, a silent invitation. Her eyes flicked to her friend, and I could hear the whisper, "That's Ricky. He's bad news." She shook her head and said, "No, I heard about you," torn between what she was being told and what she felt.

I leaned back, a smirk playing on my lips. The worst part? I knew she wanted to come over. Her friend was just trying to block my blessing. But now, now that I'd seen her again, I wasn't about to let her slip away so easily. I knew where she hung out, and I knew I'd be seeing her again.

And when I did, no amount of whispering was going to keep me from what I wanted.

11

"Summer, Summer, tiiiiime." That new DJ Jazzy Jeff and Fresh Prince drifted through the park, blending with the laughter and chatter of families scattered across the grass. As Shaun and I pulled up to McKinley Park, the music hit me with a wave of nostalgia. It was the kind of day that made you want to soak up every second, where the air was thick with the scent of BBQ and the sun seemed to hang in the sky just a little longer.

Shaun's girl had roped him into coming because her family was all about some baseball and BBQ today, that classic summer vibe. As soon as I stepped out of the car, I felt the energy—kids running wild, grills sizzling, and people lounging around, blunts blazing, drinks being poured, people on blankets, just enjoying the day. I made my way around, throwing out handshakes and hugs, feeling the love from all sides.

Then, out of the corner of my eye, I spotted my brother. He was chilling on a bench with his girl, but what really caught my attention was the girl sitting next to them. Maybe it was the way the sunlight played off her sandy hair or the easy smile she had as she talked with my brother's girl. Whatever it was, it had me hooked.

I was just about to make my move when I heard someone call out, "Erin!" I glanced over and saw her jogging to the field, a smile on her face that made the whole park seem a little brighter. So that was her name—Erin. It fit.

We ended up on opposite teams for the baseball game, and from the first pitch, I knew she was no rookie. Erin stepped up to the plate and knocked the ball into the outfield like she was aiming for the moon. Then she took off, rounding first base like a flash of lightning.

"Damn," I muttered, watching her fly around the bases. She was fast—too fast. I wasn't about to let her show me up, though. As she closed in on third, I made my move, sprinting across the field to cut her off. Instead of making the smart play and just tagging the base, I went all out and tackled her to the ground.

We hit the dirt hard, a cloud of dust kicking up around us. Erin lay there, eyes closed, and for a moment, I panicked. Had I gone too far? But then she opened her eyes, blinking up at me with a mix of surprise and irritation.

I scooped her up, trying to play it cool. "Hey, I'm Ricky," I said, flashing my best smile, the one that usually got me out of trouble. She looked at me like I was crazy. "What the hell is wrong with you?" she snapped, wincing as she noticed the scrape on her knee. Blood trickled down her leg, and her clothes were streaked with dirt.

"Didn't mean to tackle you like that," I said, helping her over to the bench. "Just got caught up in the game, you know?"

Erin wasn't having it. "You didn't mean to? What, does that make it better?" she fired back, clearly annoyed.

I grabbed a water bottle and some napkins, trying to clean up the mess I'd made. "Look, let me make it up to you," I offered. "How about I take you to Suzie's for a burger? Or I can drop you off at home, maybe even swing by a store if you want to change out of those dirty clothes."

She hesitated, her expression softening slightly. "Fine," she finally said, "but only because I'm starving." We headed to my car, the silence between us thick with tension. The drive to her place felt longer than it was, each block dragging by as I wondered if I'd blown my chance. When we got there, she hopped out and disappeared inside, leaving me to wonder if she'd come back out at all.

But a few minutes later, the door opened, and she stepped out, looking like she'd just walked out of a daydream. Erin had swapped her dusty clothes for high-waisted jeans and a simple t-shirt that hugged her just right. Her hair was pulled back, and she smelled fresh, like daisies after a summer rain. I couldn't help but stare, feeling like I'd known this girl forever, even though I'd just learned her name.

She caught me staring and raised an eyebrow. "What?" she asked.

"Nothing," I said quickly, starting the car. "You just clean up nice."

She rolled her eyes but didn't hide the small smile tugging at the corners of her mouth. "So, Suzie's?"

"Suzie's," I confirmed, pulling out onto the street.

The drive to Suzie's was a lot easier, the earlier tension giving way to a more relaxed vibe. We started talking, the conversation flowing as naturally as the summer breeze. Erin was sharp, quick with a comeback, and before long, we were bantering like old friends.

"You almost outran me," I teased, glancing over at her.

"Almost doesn't count," she shot back, a playful glint in her eyes.

"Maybe not, but you gotta admit, I've got skills," I said, grinning.

"Skills in tackling girls on a baseball field? Yeah, real smooth," she retorted, but there was no heat behind it this time.

When we got to Suzie's, the place was packed, as usual. The clatter of dishes and the murmur of conversation filled the air, but we managed to snag a booth in the corner. Erin slid in across from me, her eyes scanning the room like she was taking everything in, but I caught her sneaking glances at me when she thought I wasn't looking.

We ordered burgers and fries, the classics, and by the time the food arrived, the awkwardness had faded. It felt like we'd known each other for years, even though we were still just feeling things out. The conversation flowed, easy and unforced, with that spark of something neither of us was willing to admit yet.

"So, Ricky," Erin said, leaning back in her seat with her arms crossed, like she was trying to put some distance between us even though there was none. "You always bring girls here for burgers and fries? Or am I special?"

I smirked, wiping the corner of my mouth with a napkin. "Depends. You feel special?"

She rolled her eyes, but there was a hint of a smile. "Smooth," she said, shaking her head. "Real smooth."

"Hey, I'm just sayin'," I replied, shrugging. "Figured you'd like a place that's not trying too hard. Besides, the food's good, and the company..." I paused, looking at her, "...well, that's what really matters, right?"

She took a sip of her soda, her eyes never leaving mine. "You got a reputation, you know," she said, her voice light but with an edge. "People talk."

I leaned forward a bit, resting my elbows on the table. "And what exactly are they saying about me?"

She smiled, but it didn't quite reach her eyes. "Oh, you know... that you're trouble. Bad news." Her gaze held mine for a second longer than necessary. "I'm not trying to get caught up in all that."

I laughed softly, shaking my head. "Look, I won't lie. I've made my mistakes. But people like to talk more than they know."

She raised an eyebrow. "You really expect me to believe you're just misunderstood?"

I leaned back, my hands up in mock surrender. "I'm not asking you to believe anything. I'm just saying... get to know me before you write me off."

Erin's eyes flicked to the side, as if she was considering it, but she wasn't ready to let me off that easy. "I've seen guys like you before," she said, her voice softer now. "You make a lot of promises, but when things get real, it's all talk."

"That's the thing," I said, my voice dropping lower, more serious. "I don't make promises I can't keep."

She studied me for a moment, like she was trying to figure out if I was for real or just putting on a show. There was a wall between us, and I could tell she wasn't about to let it down easily. But beneath all that, I caught something—curiosity, maybe even interest, though she wouldn't admit it.

"So, what's your plan then, Ricky?" she asked, tilting her head. "You just here to mess around, or is this some kind of game to you?"

I smiled, but it was softer this time, not cocky. "Nah. No games. I don't know where this goes, but I'm not just here for fun."

Erin took another bite of her burger, pretending like she was thinking it over, but I could see through it. She was playing hard to get, but there was something in her eyes—something that said she'd had her eye on me long before tonight.

"You're not making it easy," I said, leaning back and watching her.

"Good," she shot back, wiping her fingers on her napkin. "Why should I?"

"I like a challenge," I said, grinning.

She shook her head, trying to hide her own smile. "You think you're so smooth, don't you?"

"I just know what I want," I replied, holding her gaze.

The conversation kept rolling from there, playful, but with a deeper undercurrent neither of us wanted to fully acknowledge. She wasn't ready to let me in, but I wasn't about to give up. Somewhere between the bites of greasy burgers and sips of soda, I realized I didn't want the night to end. Erin was different—she made me think about things I usually tried to ignore. The future, maybe even something real. And from the way she was looking at me, I had a feeling she was wondering the same thing, even if she wouldn't say it out loud.

When we finished our food, I stood and extended my hand to her. There was no hesitation—she took it, like she knew I wasn't just offering, but expecting it in some way. We walked back to the car, her hand still in mine, the silence between us comfortable.

I stopped at the passenger side, pulling the door open, making sure she noticed the gesture. I glanced from her to the seat, giving her a look that said, *I'm ready when you are.* She smiled, a soft acknowledgment, and slid in. I closed the door gently, then made my way around to the driver's side, the small win not lost on me.

"So, Ricky," Erin said, leaning back in her seat, her eyes sparkling with mischief. "Is this your usual move? Tackle a girl to get her attention?"

I laughed, shaking my head. "Only when it's worth it. Figured it was the quickest way to make you notice me."

"Well, mission accomplished," she said, smirking.

On the drive back, the conversation was lighter, the silences comfortable. We were in a good groove, and I found myself hoping this wouldn't be the last time we hung out. When we pulled up to her place, she paused before getting out.

"You know," she said softly, "You're not as bad as people say."

"And you're not as mad as you pretended to be," I shot back, earning a small laugh.

She opened the door, stepping out, but before she closed it, she looked back at me. "Maybe we can do this again sometime. Without the tackling."

"Deal," I said, watching as she walked up to her door, my heart still racing from the day.

As I drove away, I couldn't help but smile. Erin was different, in a way that made me want to stick around and find out more.

12

"If I ain't got you with me, baabbyyyyy!" Alicia Keys' soulful voice echoed through the stereo as we rolled down Franklin Blvd. The sun dipped low, casting a golden hue across the pavement. I eased the car to a stop in front of Caballo Blanco, my favorite spot to grab a bite. My hand naturally found its place on Erin's thigh, a gesture that felt as familiar as breathing. I turned to her, a smirk tugging at the corner of my lips. "This song reminds me of you," I said, and we spent the rest of the car ride feeling into the song, this moment.

"Some people want diamond rings, some just want everything, but everything means nothing…"

It's been six months—six solid months of us being inseparable. Late nights shooting pool, bingeing on Chunky

Monkey ice cream like it's going out of style—can you believe she'd never even tried it before we met? Crazy, right? Just last week, I took a trip up to Fresno to visit Aunt Ginger and all my cousins. First time in a minute I'd been without Erin, and it felt... off. I mean, she's my girl now. That's locked in, no debate. Ain't nobody got the right to even glance her way, let alone think about taking her from me.

So, while I'm up in Fresno, I'm talking to Aunt Ginger about Erin. Naturally, Aunt G wants to meet her—she's always gotta meet my girls, make sure they pass the family vibe check. I told Aunt Ginger to go ahead and give her a call, send her up on the train while I handled some business. Next thing I know, my auntie's calling Erin's house, and her mom picks up. And get this—she introduces herself as "Erin's Aunt Ginger." Man, her mom was straight-up confused. She's like, "Erin doesn't have an Aunt Ginger." My Tía is wild for that one. They've only talked on the phone a couple of times, but she's gotta get used to her, I guess. She's always been like a second mom to me, and if Erin's rolling with me, that means she's rolling with the fam too.

Over the months, I've brought Erin around to meet all my connects. Of course, I play it cool—introduce her as just a friend, nothing more. We make the exchange, hang out for a bit, then dip. But here's the wild part: not once has she asked me what I do for a living. Not once has she pried into how I make my money. We've spent hours on end, talking about everything and nothing, vibing to music, hitting up our favorite spots to eat. And still, no questions. It's like she knows there are some things better left unsaid.

That's what's so refreshing about Erin—she's got this innocence, this naivety that's rare to find. She's not trying to play the role, not pretending like she's about that life. She's just herself, and that's intriguing as hell. Any other woman would've been all up in my business, trying to figure out what I'm into, risking it all for a piece of the action. But not Erin. Her silence on the matter is almost comforting. It's like she knows what's up but chooses to live in the moment instead of prying into something that might just change the whole dynamic.

Her not asking questions? That's my assurance she ain't working with the feds. You gotta be careful out here—someone's always trying to play you, especially when you're moving weight like I am. I've seen it too many times. But with Erin, I don't get that vibe. She's pure, in her own way, and that's something I've come to respect.

The night rolled on, and we sat there, parked outside Caballo Blanco. The warm summer breeze flowed through the open windows, mixing with the scent of fresh tortillas and grilled carne asada from the restaurant. I looked over at Erin again, her face soft in the twilight. It's moments like this that make all the hustle, all the chaos, worth it. With her by my side, the world feels just a little less complicated.

"Let's eat," I said, breaking the comfortable silence. I killed the engine, and we stepped out of the car, hand in hand. Inside Caballo Blanco, the familiar faces nodded in our direction, recognizing me as a regular. But tonight, it was different—I wasn't just another face in the crowd. I was here with Erin, my girl.

As we sat down, I caught myself thinking about the future—something I rarely do. But with Erin, it's hard not to. She's got this way of making everything seem... better. More hopeful, less bleak. I don't know where this road is taking us, but for the first time, I'm not worried about the destination. I'm just enjoying the ride.

Erin's eyes lit up at the sight of the spread, and I couldn't help but chuckle. "You're gonna love this," I said, watching her dig in. She looked up at me, a playful glint in her eyes.

"Oh, am I?" she teased, tilting her head slightly. "You seem so confident, Ricky. What if I'm not impressed?"

I leaned in, smirking. "Oh, trust me, I've never let you down before, have I?"

She raised an eyebrow, biting her lip as she slowly chewed her food. "Mmm... you might be right about that."

I laughed, feeling the familiar spark between us. As she savored each bite, I couldn't resist picking up a piece and offering it to her. She smiled, leaning in closer, her lips brushing my fingers as she took the bite. Something shifted in me, something deeper than I expected.

"You trying to spoil me, huh?" she said softly, her voice laced with a playful challenge. "You know I could get used to this."

I grinned, my hand lingering near her cheek. "Maybe that's the plan. Keep you coming back for more."

She leaned in, her eyes locking with mine, and whispered, "You think you can handle that?"

There was something in her tone, something that made my pulse quicken. She wasn't just someone I cared about—she was someone I wanted to take care of, protect, make sure she never had to worry about anything. For the first time, it felt like I wasn't just looking out for myself—I was looking out for us.

"Nah," I said, my voice low. "I know I can."

13

"Ring, ring, ring!" The sound of the phone cut through the quiet of the house, breaking the evening's calm. I heard Ma in the other room, her slippers scuffing against the old linoleum as she grumbled to herself. "Who in the hell is calling this late?" she muttered, irritation lacing her voice.

She picked up the phone, her tone shifting from annoyed to protective in an instant. "Stop calling! He's married with children!" Ever since Ma met Erin, she's taken it upon herself to play bodyguard, shutting down any girl who dared to dial our number. It's like she's got a radar for trouble, always stepping in before I even know what's up.

Ma thinks she's slick, always pretending to clean the counters or shuffle around the kitchen whenever I'm on the phone. Then she'll hit me with that innocent act, asking who I'm talking to, like she didn't just catch every word. But that's just her way of keeping tabs, making sure I'm not messing up too badly.

I've been around Ma's place more often lately. No matter how far I stray, she makes sure there's always a place for me here. She's been inviting Erin over for dinner a lot, and I'm not complaining. If there's one thing me and Erin do well together, it's eating. Ma always cooks up a storm, like she's trying to remind me what I'd be missing if I ever got stupid enough to let Erin slip away.

After dinner, I felt that familiar itch—the one that tells you time's running out and there's business to handle. The clock was ticking, and I had to move. The mules had just brought back some fresh product from across the border, and it was on me to get it to the trap house on the other side of town. I don't deal with the small-time stuff anymore—it's too risky, too messy. I keep my moves clean and quick, in and out, money in hand before anyone even knows I was there.

Erin knew I had to meet up with some "friends" after dinner, and since I promised it'd be a quick run, she decided to stick around with Ma. Not that she had much of a choice—Ma was already planning their trip to Macy's before I could finish my sentence. I left some cash on the counter for them and grabbed my jacket.

Stepping out into the night, the air felt cool, almost like it was giving me a warning. The southside was buzzing tonight; the streets were alive with their usual energy. You could feel it—the tension, the anticipation, the way the city never really sleeps. I kept my head low, cruising through the blocks, my mind focused on the task at hand.

Lately, I've been doing my runs solo. Jason's been trying to keep his hands clean, and I can't blame him. He's been pushing me to get out too, to focus on something legit like getting back into DJing. I respect his hustle, and he respects mine, but I'm not ready to let go just yet. The money's too good, and I need it coming in from every angle.

"Bop, bop!" The sound of gunfire echoed through the night as I pulled up around the corner from the trap house. My grip on the wheel tightened, adrenaline kicking in. This was the life I chose, and I knew the risks, but that didn't stop the tension from creeping up my spine. I had a job to do—drop off the product, make the exchange, and then collect my money from my runners. It was supposed to be smooth, but nothing's guaranteed in this game.

I parked the car a few blocks away, killing the engine and sitting in the dark for a moment. My breath was steady, but my mind was racing, calculating every possible move. The neighborhood was too quiet, the kind of quiet that makes you second-guess everything.

I stayed in the car for a moment, scanning the area, but nothing seemed off—at least not at first glance. I couldn't shake the feeling, though. The kind that creeps up on you, makes your skin crawl, tells you something's about to go down.

I took a deep breath and pushed open the door, my breath forming a thin mist in the cool air as I moved toward the trap house, staying close to the shadows. My footsteps were soft, almost silent, but the tension in the air was loud enough to make my heart pound.

I was halfway across the street when the flashing red and blue lights cut through the darkness, painting the entire block in a wash of color. The sound of sirens followed, loud and sudden, like a switch had been flipped. My stomach dropped.

"Shit," I hissed under my breath, instinctively reaching for the gun tucked in my waistband. I stopped myself, knowing that pulling it now would only make things worse.

The police cruisers swarmed the block, blocking off both ends of the street in a matter of seconds. Doors flew open, and cops poured out, weapons drawn, their shouts echoing off the buildings. I was caught out in the open— no cover, nowhere to run.

"Hands up! Hands up!" one of the officers yelled, his voice amplified by the adrenaline pumping through the scene. I didn't have a choice. I slowly raised my hands, my heart pounding so hard I could feel it in my throat. Every instinct screamed at me to bolt, but there was nowhere to go. I was pinned down by a wall of badges and guns, and there was no way out.

"Step away from the vehicle!" another officer shouted, his flashlight blinding me as it cut through the darkness.

I took a step back, my mind racing. This was supposed to be a quick drop—get in, get out, no complications. But now the whole street was lit up, and I was right in the middle of it.

"Down on the ground!" The command came sharp and loud, leaving no room for negotiation.

I got down slowly, feeling the rough pavement scrape against my knees. My thoughts were a whirlwind, trying to figure out who tipped them off. Was it one of my runners? Someone inside the trap house? Or just bad luck? It didn't matter now. All that mattered was getting out of this alive.

The cops moved in, quick and efficient. One of them yanked my arms behind my back, slapping the cuffs on so tight they bit into my wrists. I gritted my teeth, trying to stay calm, trying not to let the anger show.

"Got anything on you we need to know about?" an officer barked, patting me down with rough hands.

"Just my wallet," I muttered, knowing they'd find nothing. They didn't know what car I came out of or exactly where I was approaching. Lucky for me, they hadn't found the ride yet. I watched from the corner of my eye as they moved around, searching for something—anything—that could tie me to the drop. But I'd been smart. The car I'd ditched around the corner? That was the key. It had enough in it to bury me for good. But I knew someone would take care of it, just like they always did.

They hauled me up off the ground and shoved me toward one of the cruisers. The lights kept flashing, turning everything into a blur of red and blue. I caught a glimpse of the trap house in the distance, the door slightly ajar, but no one was coming out. The place was dead quiet.

"Looks like we got ourselves a big fish tonight," one of the cops sneered as they shoved me into the back of the car. The door slammed shut behind me, sealing me in with the smell of sweat and old vinyl. How the hell did this go so wrong so fast? The night was supposed to be simple—just another job, just another stack of cash.

The cops were talking up front, their voices low, but I could hear the satisfaction in their tone. They thought they'd scored big tonight, but they didn't know half of it. I wasn't going down easy. I had connections, people who could pull strings, get me out of this jam. I thought back to the car—there had been at least two kilos of product in the trunk, enough to bury me under the prison for life. But that car? It would disappear. Someone in the department had already been paid off to make sure of it.

I sat in the back of the cruiser, staring out the window as the cops talked like they'd just bagged a trophy. What they didn't realize was the evidence they were so sure of was already gone. No car, no product, no case. One phone call, and it'd all be wiped clean. I wasn't untouchable, but I wasn't stupid either. My crew had already set things in motion before I even hit the pavement.

I knew the game, knew how the system worked. The cops thought they had me, but I wasn't sweating it. One of my boys had slipped the right person enough cash to make sure this didn't stick. It wasn't the first time, and it wouldn't be the last. By morning, the car would be gone, along with everything inside it. All they'd have on me was being in the wrong place at the wrong time, and my lawyer would make that disappear too.

The night was far from over, but the game had just changed. And as much as I hated to admit it, Jason's words were echoing in my head. Maybe it was time to start thinking about an exit plan. Because in this life, the only guarantees were a jail cell or a grave, and I wasn't ready for either.

14

I jolted awake to the sound of metal clanging against metal, the familiar echo bouncing off the cold, concrete walls. "Folsom State Prison," I muttered under my breath, shaking off the remnants of sleep. It had been 22 days, and I was starting to get the hang of the routine in here, but that didn't make it any easier. Each day felt like a year, and every face in here had a story, most of them ugly.

Breakfast in this place was about as appetizing as you'd expect—soggy eggs, rubbery bacon, and something they called oatmeal. The smell alone was enough to turn your stomach, but you learn quick that you either eat or go hungry. I grabbed my tray and made my way over to sit with the boys. In here, alliances are everything. You stick to your people, or you find yourself on the wrong side of something real quick. As I picked at my food, I glanced up and caught sight of someone familiar across the room. It was my boy Don. We hadn't seen each other in a minute, and now here he was, locked up in the same place as me. We grew up together, ran the streets together, and even pimped hoes together. I had to go over and say what's up. Out in the streets, I didn't care what color you were as long as you were solid, and I wasn't about to change that in here.

Don was sitting with the black crew, and I was with the Mexicans, but that didn't matter to me. I stood up and started walking toward him, and he did the same. As we met in the middle, you could feel the tension in the room rise. Both sides were eyeing us like we were about to start some shit, but that's not how I roll. We dapped each other up, exchanged a few quick words, and then went back to our tables. When I sat back down, the Mexicans started giving me grief about talking to the so-called "opps," but that's just not my style. I respect the lines in here, but I'm not about to turn my back on a lifelong homie.

Later, out in the yard, the tension was still thick. Everyone seemed ready to beef over what went down in the chow hall. That's when Sueno stepped up. He was a quiet dude, but he made shit happen. In so many ways, he reminded me of myself, like I was looking in a mirror. He was calculated, moved with intention and logic, and not on pure emotions. Honestly, sometimes I could use some of that. He wasn't looking to throw down—he was looking to squash the beef.

He came up to me, nodded. "Ricky, right?" His voice was low, steady.

"Yeah, that's me," I said, sizing him up. "And you?"

"Sueno," he said, shaking my hand. "Saw what happened earlier. Look, man, this isn't worth it. You tryna handle business or you tryna stay stuck in here?"

I raised an eyebrow. "You think they'll let it slide?"

Sueno shrugged, his eyes sharp. "They ain't gotta. You handle your business, but don't feed into the bullshit. That's how you get caught up."

I nodded, intrigued by the way he carried himself. "You always think like that? All logical?"

He gave a short laugh, almost under his breath. "You gotta, man. Ain't about playing tough. I'm tryna get out, not add more time."

"What you in for?" I asked, curious now.

"Got caught up on some dumb shit," he said, not going into details. "Ain't trying to repeat that. I just want to get back home, keep it moving. All this"—he gestured at the yard—"this ain't it for me. You?"

I leaned back against the wall. "Nah, this ain't it. But it's hard to stay out of the drama, you know?"

"Yeah, I know," Sueno said, his voice serious. "But you can't let this place define you. Keep your head down, handle what you need to, and get out. That's the only way."

I respected how he wasn't trying to act tough or sell a story. He was just real. "Loyalty's important though, right?" I asked, testing where he stood.

Sueno looked me dead in the eyes. "That's all there is, man. But loyalty don't mean getting dragged into every little beef. You gotta be smart. I ain't here for anyone else but my people on the outside. You down?"

I nodded. "Yeah, I'm down. Same mindset."

He gave a small nod, like we understood each other now. "Good. Then let's not make this harder than it has to be."

No corny shit, but it felt like we'd known each other our whole lives, like we were brothers from another mother or something. I know he knew who I was from the way he came up to me and introduced himself. I had people everywhere, and my people were always taken care of. He didn't open up right away, but over time, the pieces of his story started coming out. I could see it in his eyes before he even said a word—he'd been through it. His moms and pops couldn't hold it together, split up when he was just a kid. Then, when he hit 12, she just bounced, left him hanging. His pops tried to make something out of nothing, but we both knew how that goes.

I didn't need the details to know what it felt like—having someone you trust just vanish, leaving you drowning in all these messed-up feelings you don't wanna deal with. So you do what you gotta do: shove it down, keep it moving. By the time yard time was over, we were on the same wavelength, finishing each other's sentences like we'd known each other for years.

Sueno calmed the Mexicans down, reminding them that Don had been my boy since day one, long before any of us were wearing prison blues. He laid it out straight—if anything went down, they needed to remember who had always had their back. The tension eased after that, and we spent the rest of the yard time just kicking it. But peace in here is like a fragile truce. You blink, and it's gone.

Over the next few months, me and Sueno became tight. Every morning, we'd wake up, hit the workout circuit, and then head off to our jobs. He was doing line work, while I decided to try my hand at barbering. When Sueno found out, he asked if I'd ever cut hair before. Truth was, I hadn't, but I wasn't about to let that stop me. I started putting in work, learning on the job, and before long, the homies were lining up for cuts. The Mexicans preferred coming to me over the black barbers, which helped me keep my hustle going and my head above water.

A few weeks later, I had a run-in with this big dude from the yard. He was one of those guys who thought he owned the place, always flexing his muscles and throwing his weight around. We'd crossed paths a few times, but that day, something about his vibe just rubbed me the wrong way. Maybe it was the way he was eyeing me, or maybe I was just tired of the constant posturing. Either way, it didn't sit right with me. After we exchanged a few words, things got heated fast. My fists clenched, and I could feel the blood pumping in my ears, the urge to throw down almost overwhelming.

I knew this could escalate into something serious, and the more I thought about it, the more I wanted to make sure I wasn't caught slipping. That evening, I got with Sueno and let him know I needed a piece because I was going to handle this before he did. The big dude was all talk, but I wasn't taking any chances. If this was going to go down, I wanted to be ready.

Sueno looked at me, his face serious. He didn't say anything at first, just took a deep breath and let it out slowly, like he was choosing his words carefully. "You really want to go down that road, homie?" he asked, his voice calm but firm. "You know where that leads, right? More time, more heat, and a whole lot of regret. We got a date, man. We're almost out of here. Don't mess that up over some petty bullshit."

His words hit me hard. I could feel the anger bubbling under the surface, but Sueno's calm cut through it like a knife. He was right. I didn't want to admit it, but he was. There was no point in throwing away everything I'd worked for just because some dude in the yard couldn't keep his ego in check. I nodded, the adrenaline fading, replaced by the reality of the situation. I didn't need a piece; I just needed to keep my head down and focus on getting out.

"Thanks, man," I said, meaning it. Sueno had a way of cutting through the noise and bringing things into perspective. He clapped me on the back, a small smile on his face.

"Anytime, bro," he replied. "We're in this together. Just remember, the streets'll be waiting for us when we get out. Seven more days, man. Let's make sure we actually get there."

And with that, I knew what I had to do. Keep my head low

15

The heavy, metallic clang of the prison gates echoed in my ears, just like it did on my first day inside. But now, it was different—now, it was the sound of freedom. Four months might not seem like much, but when you're on the inside, every day feels like a year. I'd made it out clean, thanks to a slick lawyer my momma found. The bust was big, the kind that usually buries you deep, but they couldn't pin me to anything solid. No real evidence, just whispers and suspicions. That's how I walked out with a deal that felt like a second chance.

I stepped out into the blazing sunlight, squinting as it hit me. The same oversized gray and red sweatsuit I had picked up from Oxford Street before coming in now fit snug on my frame—I'd been putting in work in here. I'll never let a day go to waste, in or out. I didn't look back as I walked across the lot, eyes locked on a tan '72 Cutlass Supreme parked at the curb. I had bought it for Erin right before they hauled me away. Seeing that ride brought a smile to my face, but it was Erin's presence behind the wheel that really made my heart jump.

She took the news of my hustle better than I expected. When the cops started snooping around, asking questions, I knew I had to come clean—at least, a little bit. I had to prepare her for the heat that was coming, the kind that could drag her down with me if she wasn't careful. "Ricky," she said, her voice steady but firm, "I don't want to know about your business dealings. I don't want to hear a thing because I'm not a good liar, and I'm not going to jail. I'm not one of those girls."

In that moment, we came to an understanding—an unspoken deal. I'd keep the hustle far away from her, make sure she was always good, and in return, she'd stand by me, but never get involved. That's how it had to be.

I slid into the passenger seat, leaning back in the worn leather as Erin drove off. First stop was my ma's place. You know how it is—no matter what, your momma always got your back. My momma loves me unconditionally, and I'd do anything for her, anything to keep that look of worry off her face. She didn't care what I'd been up to, just that I was home, safe and sound. The house smelled like fresh-baked cornbread and fried chicken, her way of welcoming me back, as if I'd just returned from a long trip and not a four-month stretch in Folsom.

But I couldn't hang around too long. There were things that needed handling, and the streets don't wait for anyone. After stuffing myself with my momma's cooking, I slipped out and headed straight to my stash spot. One thing I'll never be is broke. I had a pillowcase filled with about $30k that needed moving. I wasn't about to sit on that kind of cash right after getting out. Too hot. Jason was the only one I trusted with something like this. He wasn't deep in the game like me, but he understood the hustle. I knocked on his door, and when he saw that pillowcase, his eyes went wide.

"Man, you've only been out 30 days, and you already got this kind of paper?" he asked, shaking his head in disbelief. "You sure you wanna keep this up?"

He was halfway out of the game, one foot in the streets and the other in a more stable life, trying to balance that line for the sake of his kid. I could see the doubt in his eyes, but I didn't have the luxury of doubt. I was all in, and that's the only way I knew how to play it. Jason held the cash for me, even though it made him nervous, and I could tell he was second-guessing his choices.

A few days later, I picked up Jason, and we headed south. We pulled up to this rundown house, the kind that looked like it should've been condemned years ago—windows boarded up, the door barely hanging on its hinges. But I knew better. This wasn't just some abandoned spot; it was the heart of an operation, the kind of place where money was made fast and quiet.

Jason glanced at me, unease written all over his face. He never did understand why I chose to operate in the grimiest spots, the places where you couldn't trust anyone. But that's where the real money was. No eyes, no questions, just business. I reached under my seat and grabbed my piece, tucking it into my waistband. In places like this, you couldn't afford to let emotions get in the way. It was all about logic, about survival.

We circled the block, parked behind the house, and entered through the back. The connect was already waiting, his face hard as stone, not a hint of warmth in his eyes. He laid out the product on the table, bricks of methamphetamines that could flip into serious cash. I could feel Jason's hesitation, but I ignored it. This was the game, and I was a player.

"This is the stuff that makes you quick money," I said, nodding toward the bricks.

Jason ran the cash through the counter, the steady beep of the machine cutting through the silence. I sent him out to bring the car around while the connect and his crew strapped the product under the chassis. Everything moved like clockwork, no wasted motion, no unnecessary talk.

Back in the car, Jason looked at me, his expression tight.

"Ricky, you're really doing it out here," he said, his voice low. "But I can't get behind meth. I've already lost enough time with my son. If I get locked up again, it's over for me."

I nodded, understanding where he was coming from. He had something to lose, something real. I respected that. But me? I wasn't there yet. My hustle was all I had, and until I found something else, I was gonna keep pushing.

Someday, I might look at things differently, but for now, this was the life I chose. And I was damn good at it.

16

The sound of a creaking floorboard jolted me awake, adrenaline surging through my veins. I shot up, heart pounding in my chest like a relentless hammer. The familiar scent of stale smoke and cheap cologne filled my nostrils, a reminder of where I was—Lemon Hill trap—a place where time seemed to stop, but the world outside kept spinning, indifferent to our existence. The room was dim, the first light of dawn barely creeping through the torn blinds. I reached for my phone, the screen glowing with missed calls—fifteen of them—all from Erin.

"Shit," I muttered under my breath, running a hand through my damp hair. The pit in my stomach grew as I scrolled through the missed calls, each one more urgent than the last. This was the side of the life she wasn't used to, but she would have to get used to it. When you're putting in work, distance is a must. But the calls, the endless texts—it was her way of holding on, of reminding me that there was more to this life than just survival.

I sighed, the weight of my choices pressing down on me. As I pulled on my jeans, the guilt started creeping in, slow and insidious. Erin wasn't like the other girls who clung to me when I was on the streets. She was different— steady, solid. But even she was feeling the strain of my absence, of the life I led. I'd been in the pen for months, and in that time, my priorities had shifted—reorienting themselves around survival, money, and making sure the streets hadn't forgotten me. But in doing so, I'd started to forget the people who mattered the most.

I slipped out of the trap house, the early morning air cool against my skin. The sky was a murky gray, the sun still struggling to break through the clouds. I hopped in the Camaro, the engine growling to life, and headed straight for Mack. The streets were quiet, the calm before the storm, but my mind was anything but.

Erin stood on the porch, her eyes scanning the street. When she saw me, relief washed over her face, but it was tinged with something else—something deeper, like fear or uncertainty. Her mom was right behind her, arms crossed, eyes narrowed, watching me like a hawk. I didn't need this right now—the last thing I needed was to be lectured.

"Where you been?" Her mom's voice cut through the warm evening air, sharp and accusatory. But before I could even open my mouth, Erin was already moving. She waved her mom off, sliding into the passenger seat, her movements quick and tense. I could tell her mom wasn't fooled—she knew what I was about, and she didn't like it.

As I peeled away from the curb, the tension in the car was thick, almost suffocating. The silence stretched between us, heavy with unspoken words. I could feel her eyes on me, and I knew what was coming. I braced myself, gripping the wheel tighter as I glanced at her. She was looking at me, her face a mix of worry and frustration, her brows furrowed as if trying to figure out what to say.

"Ricky, where the hell have you been?" Her voice cracked, and I could hear the pain in it, the hurt she was trying to mask. She wasn't just asking about the last week— she was asking about us, about what we were becoming. "I've been calling you all week!" She paused, struggling to find the words. She bit her lip, her eyes glistening as she finally said, "I'm pregnant."

The world around me froze. The sounds of the city, the hum of the engine—everything faded into the background as her words echoed in my mind. My hands tightened on the wheel, knuckles white. This was it—the moment that was supposed to make me rethink everything, to make me want to put the streets behind me. I was going to be responsible for another life, for a tiny human who would depend on me for everything. But instead of feeling the weight of that responsibility, all I could think was, *I gotta go harder.*

The streets have a way of blurring time, of making months feel like days and days like hours. Maybe it was the thought of being a dad, or maybe time was just slipping through my fingers, but suddenly, everything felt like it was moving too fast. I wanted to get this right—to be the father mine never was. But I knew it wasn't going to be that simple. I couldn't just walk away from the life I'd built, from the streets that had shaped me. I needed to find a way to balance it all, to provide for my family while still keeping my edge.

A house—that's the first step. Erin's got a legit job, and I've got the cash. A spot down the street from her mom's just went up for sale—a three-bedroom townhouse with a detached garage. Perfect for keeping her close to family but giving us the space we needed.

We spent the next week covering paper trails, making sure the money was clean. I couldn't afford to have anything traced back to us, not with a baby on the way. Two weeks later, it was ours. Move-in day came fast—a whirlwind of boxes, plans, and a sense of something new, something real. Erin wanted custom closets in every room, talking about how she'd always dreamed of organizing baby clothes and toys. I could see the excitement in her eyes, a glimpse of the life she wanted for us. While she focused on the details, I was more concerned with finding spots to stash cash— behind picture frames, inside kitchen chairs, even in the freezer, wrapped in foil like leftovers. If anything happened to me, my family wouldn't want for anything. This wasn't just about surviving; it was about securing a future.

That first night in the new place, as we settled into bed, I rubbed Erin's belly—barely showing yet, but the thought of what was growing inside her gave me a sense of something I couldn't quite name. Her body relaxed against mine, and just as I felt her drift off, she startled awake. I frowned, turning to her, "What's wrong, mama?"

She didn't answer right away, but the look on her face told me everything. Her eyes were wide, her breathing uneven, like she'd just had a nightmare she couldn't shake off. "C'mon Erin, I know you. Something's up."

She hesitated, then started, her voice shaky. "I've been having these dreams... but this one was different. I can't explain it."

I stayed silent, letting her talk, knowing she needed to get it out.

"I saw our little girl," she whispered, her voice tinged with something close to awe. "This baby, it's a girl, Ricky. We were so happy, a real family. But then... There was this woman, or something, made of smoke. She kept trying to pull you away. I kept telling you to stay, but you just said, 'I'll be right back.' And then... you didn't come back."

Her voice trembled, and she confessed, "I've had this dream more than once. It's like she's trying to take you from us."

Her words hung in the air, heavy and unsettling. I didn't know what to say; I didn't know how to comfort her. But one thing was clear—we were having a little girl. And I was going to be a dad. The thought filled me with both dread and determination. I pulled her closer, wrapping my arms around her, the weight of responsibility settling in my chest.

Daddy's about to have a little girl.

17

I never mess with the radio. It's usually just noise, but today, something made me turn it on. As soon as I did, I was hit with a voice singing, "A Sinner's Prayer." I'm not one for church or gospel, but this cat, Deitrick Haddon, he had a way of making you feel every word. Erin's always been the one praying for me, and I'm sure she'd say this was a sign. I'm skeptical, but there's something about this song that sticks. I decided to head over to Fry's and pick up the CD.

As I drive, the lyrics keep playing in my head, "I could've been dead, sleeping in my grave, but God rescued me, to see another day..." The words hit different, like they're meant for me. This is the type of music that could save a soul. I take the disc out and think, this is what I'm gonna play when my baby girl's here. I want her to grow up with something good in her ears, something pure.

I'm pulling up to the garage when it opens on its own, and there's Erin, waving at me like she's got some sixth sense. "How'd you know I was here?" I ask, raising an eyebrow.

She smiles that knowing smile, the one that makes me think she's from another planet. "I told you, whenever you're close by, I always hear the song play, 'Just in case, I don't make it home tonight.' That's my cue to check for you, and you're always right here. We're connected, Ricky."

She's something else, man. I was just stopping by the house to grab my piece and some cash for a deal I needed to make later. I don't even turn the car off, just kiss her cheek and drive off.

I head up North, pulling up at an old friend's place. Every time I come through, this girl Dee is all over me. She's got this energy—smooth, magnetic, like something dangerous wrapped in silk. Her skin is deep, rich chocolate, gleaming under the dim light, and her eyes… they seem to see more than what's in front of them, like she's carrying some kind of dark secret. There's a mystery to her, something almost too alluring, like she's casting a spell with every glance. I won't lie, I like the attention. I'm not looking to wife her up or anything, but the way she flirts—it's the kind of thing I've dealt with my whole life. Women throw themselves at me, eating up whatever dreams I'm selling.

Normally, I'd roll a blunt, we'd all smoke, and chill before heading out. But this time, Dee brings out this black box, moving with a slow, deliberate grace that makes my stomach twist, like something's off. I squint, trying to read the label as she sets it on the table. An Ouija board.

"You believe in this?" she asks, her lips curling into a playful smirk that doesn't quite match the shadow in her eyes.

"Nah," I shrug. "People move those things themselves."

Her grin spreads wider, a glint in her eye that sends a shiver down my spine. "Let's play."

This chick is wild, but I've never been one to back down, so I'm in. Dee's fingers, long and delicate, almost glide over the planchette like she's done this before. "Is there a spirit here with us?" she asks, her voice low, sultry, like she's inviting something unseen. The planchette drags itself to "Yes," and I'm convinced she's pushing it.

"Do you have a message for me?" she asks, her tone sweet, but there's an edge to it, something that makes the hair on the back of my neck stand up. Again, it moves to "Yes." She doesn't look scared, though. If anything, she's more alive now, her eyes shining. But then, the board jerks—moves like something's taken over. I lean in, trying to catch her in the act.

"You're moving it," I accuse, my voice harsher than I meant. But she swears she's not, and for the first time, there's a flicker of uncertainty in her eyes. The planchette drags itself across the board, slow and deliberate, spelling, "H-O-R-R-I-B-L-E D-E-A-T-H."

We all read it together: "Horrible death." The room gets colder, tighter. Dee's smirk fades, replaced by something darker, a shadow creeping into her expression. But I haven't had my turn yet. I place my fingers on the planchette, feeling its icy surface, almost like it's alive under my touch.

"Do you have a message for me?" I ask, keeping my voice steady, though my gut tells me to back off. At first, nothing happens. Just as I'm about to pull away, the board jerks again, the planchette moving faster this time, spelling out: "P-R-I-S-O-N F-O-R L-I-F-E."

No one says it out loud this time, but we all see it. My heart's racing. I let go of the planchette like it burned me. I didn't even say goodbye. I just jumped in the Camaro and peeled out of there, my foot heavy on the gas. I got from the North to the South in ten minutes, so fast that Erin didn't even have time to feel me coming home. When I walked through the door, I must've looked like I saw a ghost because Erin's eyes went wide. "Ricky, you look like you've seen a ghost," she said, half-joking, but I wasn't laughing.

I took a deep breath, trying to steady my nerves, and told her everything—about Dee, her cousin, the Ouija board, and the message it spelled out. Erin's face went from disbelief to worry in seconds. "Why were you playing with that? Do you know the kind of spirits you allow in your life messing with things like that and people like that?"

She was right, and I knew it. I was spooked enough to ask her to pray for me right then and there. I wasn't one to pray, but if there was ever a time I needed it, it was now. As she prayed, I felt some of that weight lift off my shoulders, like a cold wind blowing through the room, clearing out the bad vibes.

Afterward, Erin turned on "The Bold and the Beautiful," her comfort show. We sat there on the couch, the tension slowly draining from the room. One of the main characters popped up on screen—a woman with striking green eyes.

Erin's face lit up. "That's it," she said, suddenly excited. "Let's name her Zoe."

I looked at the screen, then back at Erin.

"Zow-Eee"

It had a nice ring to it. "Yeah, I like that," I agreed, and just like that, our little girl had a name.

As we sat there, the TV droning on in the background, I couldn't shake the feeling from earlier. The Ouija board, the message—it all felt like a warning. But I pushed it down, focusing instead on the future, on Erin, on Zoe. Whatever was coming, I'd face it head-on. For now, I just wanted to hold on to this moment, to this feeling of peace, no matter how fragile it was. The street life was still out there, waiting, but here, in this living room, with Erin and our unborn daughter, I felt like I could be something more. Something better. And I was going to fight like hell to make sure nothing took that away from me.

Just as I settled into that fleeting sense of peace, a noise from outside broke through my thoughts—a dull thud, followed by the unmistakable scrape of boots against gravel. My eyes snapped to the window. The dogs, who'd been lying quietly by the door, suddenly jumped up, barking furiously.

My heart raced, a cold knot tightening in my chest. I knew that sound. Something wasn't right.

I shot up from the bed, my mind scrambling to make sense of it. For a second, everything was a blur—the flickering TV screen, Erin's startled voice, the dogs going wild. I rushed to the window and pulled the curtain back just enough to peek outside. Flashing red and blue lights reflected off the glass.

My stomach dropped. **Shit.**

How could I have been so careless? In my rush to get home, I hadn't even thought—hadn't checked. And now, whatever product I still had on me was inside the car somewhere. Heavy footsteps pounded against the porch. A loud, authoritative voice boomed from outside.

"Ricky Pina! We have a warrant! Open the door!"

Panic flooded my veins as I stood frozen for a split second, my mind racing between fight or flight. There was no time, no way out. Erin called my name again, her voice tight with fear. I glanced at the hallway leading to the bedroom where she was sleeping, then back at the front door, where the shadows of officers loomed. The life I thought I could protect—this fragile peace—was crumbling around me.

And now I had to face what was coming.

18

4 years later

"Daddy!" Zoe's voice cut through the dull buzz of the prison yard like a beam of sunlight breaking through a storm. My little girl, just four years old, was a bundle of energy, sprinting toward me with a smile so bright it almost made me forget where I was. Almost. I knelt down, scooping her up in my arms as she giggled, wrapping her tiny arms around my neck.

It reminded me of the first time I laid eyes on her when she was three months old. I had gotten pictures and heard her baby coos over the phone, but the first time Erin brought her to see me, she was six months old. I'll never forget that moment.

Erin walked through the gates holding the cutest little girl I'd ever seen. She looked like a porcelain doll—fair satin skin, grayish-blue eyes like the sky after a rainstorm, with the sun just starting to break through, and dark, silky hair with soft little curls brushing her forehead.

She wore this old-fashioned white dress with the tiniest pink bow in the center of the delicate collar, and I knew we had been dropping stacks at Macy's. But that's why I sent the money—I wasn't trippin'. I wanted the best for my baby girl. For both of them. For the first time, I didn't immediately see Erin. All I could focus on was Zoe. There she was, this tiny, perfect human I helped bring into the world. Instinct took over, and I reached out to hold her, like I had known her my whole life. I cradled her gently in one arm, my finger tracing the soft curve of her cheek. And then, as if she already knew who I was, she wrapped her tiny, innocent hand around my finger. In that moment, time stopped. There was this rush of warmth, a sense of completeness I'd never felt before. But at the same time, it broke me. I felt whole having her in my arms, but incomplete knowing I'd be spending so much time away from her. It was like a piece of me had been put back together, but with a constant ache that I'd miss out on so much.

"Hey, babygirl," I whispered, my voice catching in my throat. It hurt to realize that I'd spent more time in this place than with her, that her memories of me were more of cold walls and metal bars than of a real home.

Erin followed behind, moving slower, more deliberate. Her eyes were tired, and the smile she forced didn't quite reach them. She wasn't the same woman I'd met all those years ago—the one who looked at me like I was her world. Now, I was more of a burden, a reminder of the life she'd never asked for but got anyway. She had birthed Zoe alone, after I got set up and sent back to jail again. My ma had been there for the birth, supporting Erin, but I didn't get to see my daughter until she was six months old, in this very yard. That first time I held her, she was this tiny, fragile thing, so beautiful it hurt. And I was wearing a prison jumpsuit.

Zoe wriggled out of my arms, eager to explore, as much as a child could in a place like this.

"Go grab me a Pepsi from the machine, princess," I called after her, watching as she took off toward the vending machines at the bottom of the hill.

Erin and I stood in silence for a moment, both of us watching Zoe. When she finally spoke, her voice was low, almost a whisper.

"Ricky, you really need to change your life."

I turned to look at her, the words cutting deeper than I wanted to admit. Erin's face was a mix of frustration and sadness. She wasn't nagging—this was something more.

"She's four years old now, Ricky," she continued. "Before you know it, she's going to be able to read. Do you really want her first words to be 'Folsom State Prison'? She's going to grow up one day, and she'll be able to look you up, know everything about you. You can't hide from that."

I sighed, rubbing the back of my neck.

"I know, Erin. I know. But I'm doing what I can. Have you been getting the gifts I sent? The money?" I asked, trying to shift the conversation to something lighter.

Erin's eyes softened, but the concern didn't leave.

"Yeah, we got them. The necklace is beautiful, and Zoe loves her teddy bear and pearl earrings. But, Ricky, it's not about the money or the gifts. It's about you. Being there. Being present."

"I know," I repeated, almost defensively. "I'm getting out in a month. When I'm out, we'll do something different. I was thinking... maybe we could go to the snow. I've never been, and I think it's time I really start focusing on our family. Just… slowly, you know? Starting to do things differently."

Erin's face softened a bit more, but the weariness was still there.

"I hope so, Ricky. For Zoe's sake. For all our sakes."

As Zoe ran back with the soda, her little face beaming with pride, I couldn't help but feel the weight of Erin's words. They hung in the air, heavy, even as I tried to focus on my daughter's excitement.

"Daddy, look! I got you a Pepsi!" Zoe's voice was full of joy, completely oblivious to the tension between her parents.

"Thank you, princess," I said, forcing a smile as I took the can from her tiny hands. "You're the best, you know that?"

She giggled, her innocence like a salve on my wounded conscience. But as I looked at her, I couldn't shake the image of her older, reading about her father's life, finding out the truth that I'd been trying to bury with money and gifts.

We spent the next hour playing, as much as you could play in a place like this. Zoe told me about her school, her friends, and how she wanted to be a teacher when she grew up. And with each word, I felt the weight of the life I'd chosen press down on me harder. When the guards signaled that visiting hours were over, I felt a pang of dread. It was always the hardest part—watching them walk away, knowing I wouldn't see them for another week.

As Erin led Zoe toward the gate, my daughter turned back, waving enthusiastically.

"Bye, Daddy! See you next week!"

"Bye, princess. Be good, okay? Make sure you listen to Mommy," I called after her, my voice thick with emotion. Erin gave me one last look, a mix of hope and resignation. I stood there, watching them go, until the gates clanged shut behind them. The yard felt colder, emptier. The echoes of the other prisoners' voices seemed distant, like I was in my own world, isolated by my thoughts.

Back in my cell that night, I thought about what Erin had said. About how Zoe would one day be able to read, to know everything about me. The idea haunted me, gnawing at the edges of my mind. I didn't want my daughter growing up ashamed of her father. I didn't want her to think that this life was all there was. I had a few homies inside who had found something different, something better. They'd turned to Islam, started changing their names, praying, finding peace. They'd tried to pull me in, too, telling me about Friday prayers and how all it took was one step toward Allah, and He'd come running. I wasn't ready for that—wasn't sure if I ever would be. But their words stuck with me.

"It's all about your intention, man," one of them had said. "When you're ready, just take that first step."

Maybe it was time to start thinking about that step. About what kind of man I wanted to be when I got out, what kind of father I wanted Zoe to see. The streets had a hold on me, sure, but maybe—just maybe—it was time to start loosening that grip. As I lay on my bunk, staring at the ceiling, I thought about the snow. About taking Zoe to see it for the first time, watching her play, watching her laugh. I wanted to be there for that. I wanted to be there for her, period.

The next morning, I made my decision. When I got out, things were going to be different. I wasn't sure how, wasn't sure where to start. But I knew one thing for sure—I wasn't going to let my daughter grow up thinking her father was just another name in a prison registry.

19

Prison does something to a man—makes him see the world through a different lens. But the streets, they have their own way of dragging you back in. My first week out, I had every intention of taking Erin and Zoe to the snow, just like I promised. But as soon as I got my phone and pager back, the game called. The money was there, waiting for me, and my people had kept things moving while I was locked up. I couldn't let them down. My reputation was everything, and in this life, reputation was the currency that kept you alive.

It was midnight when I found myself cruising down the streets, a new runner I picked up from Oakland sitting in the passenger seat. She had nowhere to go, and I hadn't been home in a week. The plan was to drop her off somewhere and finally head back to Erin, but things don't always go as planned.

I looked over at the girl, her face a mix of fear and exhaustion. "You can crash at my spot for the night, but listen up—don't say a word about what you do. You're just an old friend from high school, got it? One wrong move, one wrong word, and you'll regret it. This is the life you chose."

She nodded, understanding the unspoken threats that came with this world. As we pulled up to the house, the garage door opened on its own. Erin always knew when I was close. I'm telling you, she had a sixth sense. I parked the car, and there she was, standing in the doorway with that same unreadable expression.

I got out, the girl trailing behind me like a shadow.

"Erin," I started, trying to sound casual, "this is a friend of mine from high school. She's got nowhere to go, just needs a place to crash for the night. It's only for tonight, I promise."

Erin's eyes didn't leave mine. There was no anger, no sadness, just a cold, hard stare that cut through the bullshit. "Ricky," she said quietly, her voice steady, "she's not coming into my house. I can see the spirits on her, the same ones I see on you. They're not welcome here." I felt a chill run down my spine. Erin wasn't one to play around with words like that. She believed in things I couldn't see, in energies and spirits that followed you around, weighing you down like chains. I tried to argue, to push back, but she wasn't having it.

"She's just a girl who needs help, Erin. Don't make this more than it is."

But Erin shook her head, not buying any of it.

"No, Ricky. I know what she is, and I know what you've been up to. You've been gone for a week, and you think I don't notice? You think I don't feel it every time you bring that darkness back into our home? I'm not letting her in here, and I'm not letting you bring that into our daughter's life."

I sighed, running a hand through my hair, frustrated and torn. This wasn't how I planned things. I looked at the girl, then back at Erin.

"So, what do you want me to do? Just leave her out here?"

Erin's gaze softened, just a little, but her resolve was still firm.

"I don't care what you do with her, but she's not coming inside. This house is supposed to be a safe place, a clean place, and I'm not letting you ruin that."

I knew better than to push her any further. Erin had been more patient with me than I deserved, putting up with my mess for years.

"Fine," I muttered, turning to the girl. "You'll have to find somewhere else tonight. I'll drop you off at a motel."

The girl didn't argue. She knew her place in all this, just like I did. I got back in the car, and as I drove away, I could feel Erin's eyes on me, heavy with disappointment and something else—maybe it was fear, or maybe it was just the weight of knowing that this life was tearing us apart, piece by piece.

The drive was silent, the girl not saying a word. I dropped her off at a dingy motel on the outskirts of town, slipped her some cash, and told her to lay low and that she better not do anything without me knowing. As I headed back to Erin, my mind raced with thoughts of the life I'd built, the choices I'd made. The streets had given me everything, but they were also taking it all away.

When I finally got home, Erin was sitting on the couch, the TV flickering with some late-night show. She didn't look at me as I walked in, just stared at the screen like I wasn't even there. The silence between us was thick, almost suffocating. I knew I had to change, but the pull of the streets was strong. I reached for her hand, but she pulled away, her eyes still glued to the TV.

"Ricky," she said after a long pause, her voice tired, "I don't want our daughter growing up thinking this is normal. You need to figure out what's more important—us, or the life you're living."

Her words hit me harder than any prison sentence ever could. I nodded, not trusting myself to speak. I knew she was right. I leaned back, staring at the ceiling, the weight of my choices pressing down on me. Erin was right—I had to figure out what was more important. But deep down, I knew the streets weren't done with me yet.

20

The door creaked open, and the familiar scent of green enchiladas, beans, and rice hit me like a wave. The aroma instantly transported me back to simpler times. I stepped inside, heading straight for the kitchen, where I spotted a tray of pan dulce and a steaming pot of Abuelita's hot chocolate on the counter. Ma was there in her usual spot, fussing over the stove, and as soon as she saw me, her face lit up.

"Hi, mijo," she greeted me, wrapping me in a big, warm hug. "You look so handsome. Why don't you go upstairs and shave your face? I left some extra stuff up there for you."

I nodded, smiling at her familiar fussing, and headed upstairs. As I washed up, I caught a glimpse of myself in the mirror. The face staring back at me looked older, more worn than I remembered. Time had a way of slipping by, and each glance in the mirror seemed to remind me of all that had changed.

Downstairs, the house was alive with the clattering of pots and pans, the sizzle of food on the stove, and the crackling of the fire in the living room. The air was thick with the sounds of Christmas—"Feliz Navidad" playing softly in the background, mingling with the voices of my family. It was Christmas Eve, and as always, we all gathered at Ma's house. It was our tradition, one of the few constants in a life full of chaos.

My brother was there, laughing with my tíos and tías, and of course, Erin and Zoe were already making themselves at home. Even Jason and Sueno had shown up, surprising me with their appearance. I was late, had to take care of some business, but it felt good to finally be here.

Zoe, my little girl, spotted me the moment I walked into the room. Her face lit up like the Christmas tree in the corner, and she sprinted across the room, launching herself into my arms. I scooped her up, holding her close as she settled on my lap. Ma, always ready to spoil her granddaughter, handed Zoe the karaoke machine.

"Sing for us, mija," Ma encouraged her.

And just like that, Zoe grabbed the mic and started belting out "Feliz Navidad" with all the enthusiasm of a four-year-old. "Feliz Navidad, prospero año y felicidad! I wanna wish you a Mewwy Chwistmas!" she sang, her voice filling the room.

I wished I could freeze that moment, just hit pause and hold onto it forever. This right here, surrounded by family, my little girl singing her heart out, was what life was supposed to be about. The warmth, the love, the sense of belonging—it was all so real in these fleeting moments.

But like all good things, the moment didn't last. We opened presents for what felt like hours because Zoe had more gifts than anyone else. We had to take a break halfway through, and then I sent the girls home, promising Erin I'd be there soon. But I had business to handle first.

Christmas Eve wasn't just about family and presents for me; it was also the best day of the year for moving product. Most people were at home with their loved ones, and that meant fewer eyes on the streets, fewer cops watching for anything suspicious. It was the perfect cover for bringing in a big load.

I knew I had to make it quick. I'd promised Erin I'd be home tonight, and for once, I intended to keep my word.

But this was the life I'd chosen, and keeping my reputation intact meant taking care of business, no matter what.

The streets were quiet as I made my way to the drop. Christmas lights blinked in the windows of the houses I passed, a contrast to the darkness I was heading into. I didn't like doing this on Christmas Eve, but it was part of the game. And in this game, you either played to win, or you didn't play at all.

When I pulled up to the spot, my contact was already there, waiting. We exchanged quick nods—no words were necessary. The deal went down smoothly, like it always did, but there was a nagging feeling in the pit of my stomach, a weight that had been growing heavier with each passing year.

On the drive back home, I couldn't shake the feeling. The money, the power, the respect—none of it seemed to matter as much as it used to. All I could think about was Zoe's voice, the way she sang with that innocent joy, completely unaware of the world I was wrapped up in.

When I finally walked through the door, the house was quiet, except for the soft hum of the TV in the living room. Erin was curled up on the couch, half-asleep, waiting for me. She opened her eyes as I sat down beside her, giving me that look—the one that said she was tired of all this but still holding on for our daughter's sake.

"I made it," I whispered, brushing a strand of hair from her face.

She sighed, leaning into me. "You always do. But for how long, Ricky? How long until you don't?"

I didn't have an answer for that. All I knew was that, for tonight, I was home. Tomorrow could wait. For now, I just wanted to hold onto this feeling for as long as I could.

As the night slipped away, I couldn't help but wonder how many more Christmases like this we had left. But that was a question for another time. Right now, all I wanted was to soak in this moment, to let the warmth of my family fill the cold spaces inside me. Tomorrow would bring its own challenges. But tonight, I was home.

21

I jolted awake, my heart pounding, the echoes of Erin's distressed cries still ringing in my ears.

"Aggghhhhh!" she yelled, followed by "No, no!"

It took me a second to fully shake off the sleep, my mind still foggy. I rolled over and saw Erin's face buried in her hands, tears streaming down her cheeks. My groggy brain scrambled to make sense of the situation.

"Hey, hey," I mumbled, "what's going on? What's wrong?"

Erin looked up, her eyes red and puffy. "I had a dream about you, and it wasn't good."

A nervous chuckle escaped me. Erin and her dreams—she had this uncanny knack for them, like she was tapped into some weird cosmic frequency. I always felt there was something a little magical about her. But as I looked at her, her distress was palpable.

"I'm serious, Ricky," she said. "Something really bad happened to you, and you weren't with us anymore."

I tried to piece together her words, but I was still half-asleep. "Well, what do you think that means?"

"IT MEANS YOU NEED TO CHANGE YOUR LIFE."

Those words hit me like a ton of bricks, reverberating in my head. I hadn't been home much lately, and every time I was away, I felt like I was slipping further and further. It was like being tugged in two different directions—one path felt right, but the other, the "wrong" one, always seemed to pull me in with an irresistible force.

Last Saturday, I dropped by to see my brother; it had been a while since we last caught up. No matter how much time passes, I always make sure he's in the loop about my latest car project—we've always connected over that. I was there to show off the Cougar I had just restored. I've never really taken pride in much, but this car was different; it was the car I'd always envisioned myself driving.

For years, my brother was tangled up in a tough life—drugs and street hustles were his norm. But he's found a new direction now, committed to his church, and he looked genuinely content. I was happy to see him that way. However, I couldn't see myself following in those footsteps. It's like you've gone too far down your own road to even consider a detour. He believed in change, though, and wanted that for me too. He invited me to join him at church the following day. Yet when Sunday rolled around, something just held me back.

When my brother called to check if I was coming, I lied and said Erin had left me behind. In reality, she hadn't even left the driveway. A few minutes later, she stormed into the house.

"I didn't leave," she said. "Get in the car, let's go."

Walking into the church, I felt like a fish out of water. There were familiar faces—people I'd worked with, folks who'd done business with me, and others I'd just seen around town. Maybe it was the guilt gnawing at me, but I felt like an outsider. Then the pastor called for an "altar call," which, from what I gathered, was an opportunity to ask for God's forgiveness. I wanted to move, but something deep inside kept me glued to the edge of my seat. On the outside, I seemed calm, but inside, I was waging a battle that felt like it had been raging my entire life.

I wasn't exactly religious, but I knew enough to understand that asking for forgiveness wasn't something I could afford to skip. Lost in my thoughts, I didn't notice when people began to leave. It wasn't until I caught the pastor's eyes on me from the small stage that I snapped back to reality. My brother was close, but his voice sounded distant when he said, "Come meet my pastor." His pastor—it still felt so strange to me.

I walked up, introduced myself, and suddenly, the words just started pouring out. I told him how I needed to change my life, how I was tired of being surrounded by the same people, doing the same things, feeling stuck in a cycle I couldn't break. I confessed that I was desperate to ask God for any forgiveness He could offer. So, despite the discomfort gnawing at me, I let the pastor pray for me.

The room went silent, and I felt a mix of shock and subtle support from those around me. To be honest, I didn't care much about their reactions. I was there for forgiveness, not for their approval. As I stood there, a surprising sense of relief washed over me. It was as if the constant tug-of-war within me had finally ceased, even if just for a moment.

22

It was a gloomy afternoon, the sky heavy with thick, gray clouds that seemed to press down on the city. A chill hung in the air, biting through my jacket and seeping into my bones. The streets, familiar and worn, looked almost ghostly under the dull, diffused light. I drove slowly, the steady hum of the engine a stark contrast to the chaos that had defined so much of my life. Each corner, each alley held memories of a life lived in the fast lane, where danger and excitement were constant companions.

Today, however, a different feeling nagged at me—a sense of urgency and regret. The cold seemed to heighten my awareness, making each thought, each memory, sharper and more painful.

I glanced at the clock on the dashboard. It was 2:22. My fingers absently rubbed my chin, a nervous habit I had developed over the years. Stopping at a red light, my eyes drifted to the auto body shop on the corner. I had passed it countless times, each time thinking how my street smarts and knack for fixing things could have built a legitimate business. I always looked for the fast money in everything. Every time I met a monetary goal, there was always another to follow. But in this moment, I looked at that auto body shop as something my mother and children would be proud of—something I would be proud of myself for. The thought was fleeting, just like every other moment of potential that I had let slip through my fingers.

I remembered the days when I first ventured into the streets. The thrill of making quick money had been intoxicating, overshadowing the warnings from my mother and the voices in the back of my mind telling me I could do so much more. I had been so sure of myself, so convinced that I could handle anything that came my way. But now, as I sat in my car, the weight of my choices pressed down on me.

As the light turned green, I felt an overwhelming need to go home. I couldn't remember the last time I had really spent time with my daughter, and the thought of her bright eyes and innocent smile tugged at my heart. I needed to tell her I loved her, to let her know that despite all my flaws and mistakes, my love for her was unwavering.

Lost in these thoughts, I barely noticed the figure approaching my car until it was too late. The man raised a gun and unloaded the entire clip, and to my surprise, I didn't hear a thing. The earth in that moment went silent. Darkness enveloped me, and my life flashed before my eyes, a whirlwind of memories and regrets.

I thought of my mother, the one constant source of love in my tumultuous life. Her gentle touch and soothing words had been my refuge, her unwavering belief in me a beacon in the darkest times. I could see her now, standing in our small kitchen, her face lined with worry but always managing a smile for me. Her voice, warm and soft, echoed in my mind, telling me to be careful, to make the right choices. I had brushed her off, confident that I knew better.

But my father had been a different story—a man whose love I once wanted, until it became an unattainable feeling that I didn't care to revisit. The harsh words and absence of affection had left a void that I carried into my own fatherhood. Tears welled in my eyes as I thought of my daughter. I had promised myself I would break the cycle, but life had a way of leading me astray. I could see her in my mind's eye, her little face full of hope and love, and my heart ached with the weight of my shortcomings. I remembered rushing home in the middle of the night last night just to wake her up out of her sleep and tell her that I would always love her. Such a quick moment it was almost a dream, because I never stayed around for long. And in this moment, I realized all the moments I missed chasing.

My thoughts drifted to my wife, the woman who had stood by me through the chaos and the turmoil. I had not treated her right, my actions driven by anger and frustration rather than love and understanding. I remembered the fights, the harsh words that had passed between us, the nights I had stayed out, leaving her to worry and wonder if I would come home. Now, as I lay on the cusp of death, I could hear her voice—a mixture of pain and hope—but I couldn't reach out to her, couldn't let her know that I was still here, even though I was hanging on by a thread.

I could hear her crying, pleading with the doctors to save me even though she could feel my soul slipping away. Her words broke through the fog of my consciousness, each one a dagger to my heart. I wanted to tell her I was sorry, that I loved her, but my lips wouldn't move, my voice wouldn't come. I had taken her for granted, assuming she would always be there, but now I realized how much I had hurt her, how much I had lost.

As the final moments of my life ticked away, my mind was a mixture of what-ifs and should-have-beens. I saw flashes of my childhood, the streets that had both nurtured and destroyed me, the friends who had come and gone, each leaving their mark on my soul. I saw my daughter growing up without me, my wife struggling to hold everything together, and my mother mourning the loss of her son. I saw the opportunities I had missed, the paths not taken, and the dreams left unfulfilled. I remembered the nights spent on the streets, the rush of adrenaline as I navigated the dangerous world I had chosen. The faces of those I had met along the way—some friends, some foes—blurred together in a haze of memories. I had learned so much, seen so much, but at what cost? The price of my choices had been high, too high, and now I was paying the ultimate price.

In those last moments, clarity came. I realized that love was the thread that had woven through my life, even in the midst of the chaos. My mother's love, my daughter's love, my wife's love—these were the things that truly mattered.

They were the things I had taken for granted, the things I had failed to nurture. I saw now how much I had been loved, how much I had been given, and how little I had given in return.

With a final, shuddering breath, I let go. The beeping of the heart monitor flatlined, and the room was filled with a deafening silence. My mother's sobs echoed in the emptiness as I drifted into the unknown, carrying with me the hope that in some way, my love would reach them—that they would know how much they had meant to me. I hoped that my daughter would grow up knowing that I had loved her, even if I had not always shown it. I hoped that my wife would find peace, that my mother would find solace in knowing that I had finally understood.

In the end, my life had been a series of choices—some good, many bad—but it was the love I had given and received that defined me. As darkness claimed me, I found a semblance of peace in that truth, hoping that somehow, it would be enough. My last thoughts were of my daughter's smile, my wife's touch, and my mother's unwavering faith in me. And with that, I slipped into the eternal night, carrying with me the memories of a life that could have been so much more, if only I had made different choices.

20 years later

Dear Freeman Williams,

You may not know my name but I have known yours for the last 20 years. In fact, I've considered writing or reaching out to you many times but what do you say to the man who murdered your father? That is what I keep asking myself. I've recently been informed that your parole hearing is coming up soon which has pushed me to the trajectory of this letter.

My father, Ricky Pina, would have been 53 years old this year. I have officially spent more time without him in my life than with him. The first five years he was gone

I would wait by the sliding back door waiting for him to walk through until I would snap back to reality and realize I would never see him again. I was ten years old when this all happened, the age a girl REALLY needs her father. I can truly only remember him through pictures but without them I only remember his cold unalive face. My dad loved me more than anything, I have a theory that our souls have an innate knowing of when our time on earth here is done. In fact, the night before he was murdered, he came home out of nowhere and woke me up out of my sleep just to lay with me for awhile and then asked me to come downstairs so he could sit with me awhile and the last words he ever spoke to me were, "You know I am always going to love you right? No matter what.".

I know that everything happens in Divine timing, that God's plan is bigger than all of this and as much as it hurts that my father never got to see me grow up, comfort me, watch me get married, be a mother and have the chance to be a grandfather to my kids, I know that you are somebody's baby too, that someone out there may be missing you the last twenty years. I would not be who I am today without such a tragic event like losing my father at 5 years old and I hope that you did not just serve time but that the time served you as well, that you have had time to work inward about the person that you want to be in this world. If it is any consolation, I forgive you.

— *Zoe Pina*

Milton Keynes UK
Ingram Content Group UK Ltd.
UKHW031207111124
451035UK00006B/617